Companion piece

ali smith
Companion piece

HAMISH HAMILTON
an imprint of
PENGUIN BOOKS

HAMISH HAMILTON

UK | USA | Canada | Ireland | Australia
India | New Zealand | South Africa

Hamish Hamilton is part of the Penguin Random House group of companies
whose addresses can be found at global.penguinrandomhouse.com.

First published 2022
001

Penguin Random House expresses its thanks for permission to use: extract from *New and
Collected Poems 1931–2001* by Czesław Miłosz, published by Penguin Books, copyright ©
Czesław Miłosz Royalties Inc., 1988, 1991, 1995, 2001, published by Allen Lane, Penguin Press,
2001, Penguin Classics, 2005, reprinted by permission of Penguin Books Limited; extract from
'In the White Giant's Thigh' by Dylan Thomas, copyright © The Dylan Thomas Trust,
published in *The Collected Poems of Dylan Thomas: The Centenary Edition* (Weidenfeld &
Nicolson), reprinted by permission of David Higham Associates; excerpt from 'I Work All
Day . . .' by Pier Paolo Pasolini, from *Roman Poems*, translated by Lawrence Ferlinghetti and
Francesca Valente, translation copyright © 1986 by City Lights Books, reprinted with the
permission of The Permissions Company, LLC, on behalf of City Lights Books, www.citylights.
com; and 'to start,to hesitate;to stop' by E. E. Cummings, from *E. E. Cummings Complete
Poems, 1904–1962* (W. W. Norton), reprinted by permission of W. W. Norton.

Set in 13/16pt Sabon MT
Typeset by Jouve (UK), Milton Keynes
Printed and bound in Great Britain by Clays Ltd, Elcograf S.p.A.

The authorized representative in the EEA is Penguin Random House Ireland,
Morrison Chambers, 32 Nassau Street, Dublin D02 YH68

A CIP catalogue record for this book is available from the British Library

HARDBACK ISBN: 978–0–241–54134–0
TRADE PAPERBACK ISBN: 978–0–241–54135–7

www.greenpenguin.co.uk

MIX
Paper from
responsible sources
FSC® C018179

Penguin Random House is committed to a
sustainable future for our business, our readers
and our planet. This book is made from Forest
Stewardship Council® certified paper.

for Nicola Barker

and for Sarah Wood

with love

The mild valley of those who are eternally alive.
They walk by green waters.
With red ink they draw on my breast
A heart and the signs of a kindly welcome.
Czesław Miłosz

Now curlew cry me down to kiss the mouths of their dust.
Dylan Thomas

Passive as a bird that sees all, in flight,
and carries in its heart,
rising in the sky,
an unforgiving conscience.
Pier Paolo Pasolini,
translated by Ferlinghetti & Valente

I am angry to the depths of my soul that the earth
has been so injured while we were all bemused
by supposed monuments of value and intellect,
vaults of bogus cultural riches. I feel the worth of my own life
diminished by the tedious years I have spent acquiring competence
in the arcana of mediocre invention, for all the world
like one of those people who knows all there is to know
about some defunct comic-book hero or television series.
The grief borne home to others while I and my kind
have been thus occupied lies on my conscience like a crime.
Marilynne Robinson

By hammer and hand all arts do stand.
Motto of the Worshipful Company of Blacksmiths

You choose

'Ello 'ello 'ello. Wot's all this then?

That's the voice of Cerberus, the savage mythical three-headed dog (one 'ello per head). In ancient myth he guards the dead at the gates of the Underworld to make sure none of them can leave. He's got very sharp teeth, he has the heads of snakes rising off his back like hackles and he's talking in English music-hall comedy language to what appears to be a good old British bobby, which is an old-fashioned word for a British policeman.

This British policeman, though, is from right now, he's the latest corrupt upgrade, and he's crossed the river Styx and come to the entrance of the Underworld to show each of Cerberus's heads some fun photos of himself and other uniforms doing fun things like making V signs over and adding fun racist / sexist commentary to the

3

pictures of the bodies of real murdered people which he's circulated on the fun police app he and his pals are using these days, in this land of union-jack-the-lads in the year of our lord two thousand and twenty one, in which this story, which starts with me staring at nothing in my front room on the sofa one evening imagining a meeting between some terrifying aspects of imagination and reality, takes place.

Cerberus doesn't even raise an eyebrow (and he could, if he wants, raise six at once). Seen it all before. Let the bodies pile high, more the merrier in a country of people in mourning gaslit by the constant pressure to act like it's not a country of people in mourning.

Tragedy versus farce.

Did dogs have eyebrows?

Yeah, because verisimilitude's important in myth, Sand.

I could have, if I'd wanted to know for sure, got off the sofa, crossed the room and had a look at my father's dog's head to check.

But I was past caring whether dogs had eyebrows.

I didn't care what season it was.

I didn't even care what day of the week.

Everything was mulch of a mulchness to me right then. I even despised myself for that bit of wordplay, though this was uncharacteristic, since all my life I'd loved language, it was my main character, me its eternal loyal sidekick. But right then even words and everything they could and couldn't do could fuck off and that was that.

Then my phone lit up on the table. I saw the light of it in the dark of the room.

I picked it up and stared at it.

Not the hospital.

Okay.

A number I didn't know.

It surprises me now that I even answered it. I'll have thought it'd maybe be someone my father'd worked for or worked with who'd heard what had happened and was phoning to see how he was etc. I still felt a trace of responsibility about such things. So I got my responses ready. *Not out of the woods yet. Under observation.*

Hello? I said.

Sandy?

Yes, I said.

It's me, a woman said.

Uh, I said none the wiser.

She told me her name.

My married name's Pelf but I was Martina Inglis back then.

It took a moment. Then I remembered.

Martina Inglis.

She was at college the same time as I was, same year, same course. She and I hadn't been friends, more acquaintances. No, not even acquaintances.

Less than acquaintances. I thought maybe she'd heard about my father (though God knows how she would've) and even though we hardly knew each other was maybe calling me now (though God knows where she'd've got my number) to be, I don't know, supportive.

But she didn't mention my father.

She didn't ask how I was or about what I was doing or any of that stuff people generally say or ask.

I think that's the reason I didn't hang up. There was no pretence in her.

She said she'd wanted to talk to me for some time. She told me she was now assistant to the curator at a national museum (*could you ever have imagined I'd end up doing something like that?*) and she'd been travelling back from a day-return trip abroad where she'd been sent by the museum in one of the gaps between lockdowns personally to accompany home from a travelling exhibition of late medieval and early renaissance objects an English metal lock and key mechanism, a device, she explained, way ahead of its time and an unusually good and beautiful version, quite important historically.

So she'd arrived back here in the evening and stood in line at border control for the very long time it took to reach the front of the queue of people whose passports were being checked

6

manually (most of the digital machines weren't working). Then when she finally reached the front the man behind the screen told her she'd given him the wrong passport.

She couldn't think what he meant. How was there such a thing as a wrong passport?

Ah, wait, she'd said. I know. I'm sorry, I've probably just given you the one I didn't travel out on, wait a minute.

A passport you didn't travel out on, the man behind the screen said.

I've got two, she said.

She fetched her other passport out of her inside jacket pocket.

Dual citizenship, she said.

Is one country not enough for you? the man behind the screen said.

I'm sorry? she said.

I said, is one country not enough for you? the man said again.

She looked at his eyes above his mask. They weren't smiling.

I think that's my business, not yours, she said.

He took the other passport from her, opened it, looked at it, looked at the two passports together, looked at his screen, typed something in, and she realized there were now two masked officials in uniform standing very close to her, just behind her, one on each side.

If I can just see the ticket on which you travelled here today, the man behind the screen said.

She got her phone out, scrolled it till she found the ticket, turned it and held it up towards him. One of the officials took the phone out of her hand and passed it through to the man behind the screen. The man put it down on top of her passports. Then he sanitized his hands from a bottle on the desktop.

If you'd like to step this way please, the other official said.

Why? she said.

Routine check, the other said.

They started to lead her away.

Your colleague's still got my phone. He's still got both my passports, she said.

Returned to you in due course, the one behind her said.

They took her through a door and through another door into an anodyne corridor with nothing in it but a scanner. They ran the bag with the small packing crate in it containing the lock and key mechanism, which was all the handluggage she had, through their scanner.

They asked her what kind of weapon was in the crate.

Don't be silly. It's obviously not a weapon, she said. The broader object is a lock, it was once the lock on a 16th century baronial money chest. The long object next to it isn't a knife, it's the lock's original key. It's the Boothby Lock. If you knew anything about late medieval and early renaissance English metalwork you'd know it's a very important historical artefact and a stunning example of workmanship in blacksmithery.

The official opened the packing case roughly with a knife.

You can't take it out! she said.

He took the wrapped-up lock out and weighed it in his hands.

Put it back, she said. Put it back right now.

She said this with such fierceness that the official stopped weighing it from hand to hand and rather stiffly put it back into the packing crate.

Then the other official demanded she prove she was who she said she was.

How? she said. You already have both my passports. And my phone.

So you have no hard copy of any official accreditation for transporting a national historical artefact? the official holding the packing crate said.

They tried to move her to what they called the interview room. She held on to the side of the scanner's belt with both hands, made her body as heavy as she could like protesters on the news and refused to go anywhere peaceably until they'd given her back the cracked-open packing crate and let her check that both the Boothby Lock and its key were still in there.

They shut her and the bag with the packing crate in a small room with nothing in it but a table and two chairs. The table was made of grey plastic and aluminium, same as the chairs. There was no phone on the table. There were no windows. There was no visible camera on any of the walls to which she could wave or signal, though there may well have been cameras she couldn't see *but God knows where, Sand, but people can do anything with a very small lens these days. Lenses are smaller than fruitflies now. Not that there was anything even remotely alive in that room other than me.* There was also no inside handle on the door and the door could not be coaxed open by any scrabbling at its sides; there were scratch signs and little gouges at its foot and along its edge from people's past attempts at this. There was no wastepaper basket, as she discovered after banging on the door produced no one to tell her where a toilet might be or escort her to one, and what happened next was that they left her in there for what turned out to be quite a long time.

Then they released her without any interview or explanation, gave her back her phone but kept her passports, to be *returned to you*, a woman at a reception desk on the way out told her, *in due course.*

I still haven't got either of them back, she told me. And I can't make up my mind. Either they put me in there and honestly forgot about me or they forgot about me on purpose.

Either way, I said. Quite a story. Seven hours.

And a half, she said. The whole of a working day, one that started at half four in the morning and was mostly spent standing in border control queues. But seven and a half hours. In a soulless room.

Long time, I said.

Very, she said.

I knew what I was supposed to do next. I was supposed to ask what she'd done in that soulless room for seven and a half hours. But I was at a time in my life where I was past caring, I was way past politeness and social chitchat coercion.

I held back.

I was silent for about ten seconds.

Eh, hello? she said.

I don't know how she did it but something in her voice made me feel bad for holding back.

So. What did you do in there all that time, then? I said.

Ah. Thereby hangs a tale, she said (and I could hear the relief in her voice that I'd said what I was supposed to say). That's actually what I'm calling you about. Listen. This weird thing happened. I haven't told anyone else. Partly because I can't think who else to tell. I mean, I thought about it, and I kept drawing a blank. And then last week

11

I thought, Sandy Gray. Sand from the past. From when we were at university. That's who'll know what to make of this.

Make of what? I said,

and started silently to worry, because since everything had changed, and though on the surface of things I'd kept myself going partly by pretending like the rest of us that everything was fine, if awful, in fact so much had shifted that I was pretty sure I wasn't the person I'd once been.

At first, she was saying, I sat in there doing nothing, with my hands folded in my lap. I was furious but I argued myself out of my fury. I got myself ready for whatever their interview would be about.

And then the room got quite cold, so I got up and walked around a bit, it wasn't very big, the room, I started jogging round it and because it was so small I made myself dizzy doing the jogging and turning, it's lucky I'm not the claustrophobic type.

Then I tried to open the door again. But I had nothing to open it with. I actually even thought about unwrapping the Boothby Key and using its edge, it's got an edge-prong with a little thorny hook on it, I thought I might be able to catch the underside of the door with it and see if I could persuade it. But no way, no way I'd ever be responsible for damage to the Boothby.

So then I thought, I've never really had any time alone with the Boothby, have I, or even had a chance to look at it properly.

So I got the little crate out of the bag, the crate was split open now anyway, he'd ruined it with his knife. And I lifted both pieces in their swaddling out of the crate and put them on the table, and I unwrapped the lock and put it down still in the cloth in front of me. Ah, Sand, the Boothby Lock, whoever made it had God knows what magic in his hands. Have you ever seen it?

No, I said.

Ever heard of it?

No, I said.

Google it. You'll love it. You above all people'll really get it.

A person I hardly remembered existed and wouldn't have if she hadn't phoned to remind me had kept alive enough of a version of me in her head all these years to think I'd 'get' something?

Not that Google's anywhere near, she was saying, anything like seeing it in the actual flesh, the actual metal. It's really beautiful. It's really cunning too. You could never tell by looking at it that it's even a lock, or that it has any mechanism at all inside it, never mind find how or where the key goes into it to open it. It's quite hard to find when you know where to look. It's been made to mimic a lock grown over by ivy leaves, I mean even saying the

words ivy leaves doesn't do any justice, each of
these metal ivy leaves looks so like an actual ivy
leaf, and yet you know it isn't, and it's still as if, if
you took it in your hand, you'd be able to feel it give
like you can feel the give of a real leaf. And you
look at it and you know all over again how amazing
a real ivy leaf that's growing really is. And the
tendrils, it's literally like they're actually getting
longer as you watch, they're so fine, have such a,
I don't know what else to call it, rhythm, it's as if
they're pliable, moving. And when you try to hold it
all in your eye the tendrils and the leaves seem
literally to be growing as you watch out of and over
whatever the Baron or whoever used it to lock. The
lock part, according to lock historians, is a work of
extreme toughness, and yet it looks like nothing
when you open it up and examine it, I wouldn't
dare try to uncover its mechanism myself but
people higher up the museum ladder than me say
it's one of the least pickable locks they've seen for
the time it was made, or for any time actually, with
an intricate original notch mechanism not found
anywhere else for a couple of centuries, I mean a
work of just stunning skill for the time, and metals
were generally cruder then, or they were in the part
of the country it was made, and the craft needed
for making something at this level, I mean almost
unthinkable, the tools for cutting or forming
would've been so rudimentary. Anyway I didn't

dare take it in my hands, it sat there in its cloths on the table shining under the fluorescent light in that nothing of a room and it had all the centuries of colours in its metal and it was so beautiful it made me forget, for a while anyway, how much I really had to go to the toilet.

And then my bodily needs began to assert themselves for the second time, a lot more urgent than the first, and since there'd been no answer when I'd hammered on the door the first time I began to panic about what I was going to do in there, or try not to do in there ha ha if there was no answer the second time. Which is when I heard it.

She paused.

They'd finally come back for you, I said.

No, she said. It wasn't anyone. Well, it was, someone. Just not bodily. Just – what I mean is. I could hear someone speaking, like someone was there in the room. But there *was* only me in the room. It was weird. And what it said was weird.

So I reckoned someone must be in the next room and I was hearing them through the wall, the far wall behind me, but amazingly clearly, as clearly as I can hear you now. Anyway, long story short, this is what I'm phoning you about.

To tell me you heard a weird voice through a wall, I said.

No, she said, the *voice* wasn't weird. I was never

any good at describing. You'll remember that. No, it's the thing it said, what it said, that was weird. Or, not weird exactly. But I don't know what else to call it, or what to make of it, of what it said.

What did it say? I said.

Curlew or curfew.

It said what?

That's it. That's all. Just those words.

Curlew or curfew? I said.

Like a question, she said. I think it was a woman's voice. Though it was quite a deep voice. But I think too high for a man's voice, unless it was a man who happened to have quite a high voice.

What did you say? I said.

Well I went over to the wall, and I said, beg your pardon, could you repeat that please? And it said it again. *Curlew or curfew*. Then it added: *you choose*.

What then? I said.

Well, I asked whoever it was whether there was any way they could help me or alert somebody to help me get to a toilet, she said.

Then what? I said.

That's all, she said. Nothing else. And nobody came for me for what felt like at least another hour, I'm very lucky that I have the bladder control of a much younger person.

It sounds like a wind-up, I said.

I'm not winding you up, she said. Why would I?

It happened. It did. Exactly like I've told you. I'm not winding anybody up.

No, I mean, like someone trying to wind *you* up, I said. Hidden speaker system?

Very well hidden if there was such a thing, she said. I couldn't see any audio-visual anything.

Some sort of psycho border control test? I said.

I don't know, she said. It's a mystery to me. Anyway. I'm phoning because. I can't stop thinking about it.

Well, locked in the room for so long, I said. Bullied about your passports, locked up with nothing for company except a really old, uh – lock. It's a lot.

No, not those, she said. What I can't stop thinking about is curlew. And curfew. I mean, what on earth? It's like I've been given a message, I've been entrusted with it. But what *is* the message? Sand, I can't sleep at night for thinking about how I don't know what it's supposed to mean. Worrying that I'm not up to it. I get into bed tired, really exhausted. But then all I do is lie there awake in the dark worrying that I'm missing something important, something I ought to be being way more attentive to.

You're lucky that's all that's keeping you awake right now, I said.

I mean, I know what curlew means, she said, and I know what curfew means. But I don't know what the game is here. And I lie there, and Edward's lovely and everything, but I can't tell Edward.

Why not? I said.

He's my husband, she said.

Ah, I said.

I held the phone away from me. Someone I hardly knew was trying to involve me in some kind of marital inadequacy quarrel. I hovered my finger over the hang-up button.

And I can't tell my kids. One would laugh. The other would call me a cis terf, which apparently I am. The other day they both shouted at me for full-stopping them. I don't know what my own children mean any more. And I can't tell anyone at work. They'd never trust me with an artefact again, they'd think I'm insane. A fantasist.

I looked at the phone in my hand with her voice coming out of it saying the word fantasist. But I still didn't hang up. I found I was thinking instead, quite vividly and quite unexpectedly, about the lock she'd described, with its way into itself hidden by ivy that isn't ivy, its soft cloths splayed round it unwrapped on a cheap airport table in a windowless room. Something like that might transform wherever it got placed, revealing as a whole new kind of museum even an anodyne space like the one she'd made me imagine her locked up in for seven and a half hours.

And that's when I remembered *you*, she was saying now into my ear again. Back when we were at college and you had that party trick where you could decipher dreams and read palms –

Uh, I said (because I had no recollection of reading a palm or deciphering a dream for anyone ever)

– and you were really good at sounding like you knew what a line of poetry meant, and so on. You just knew what things meant. Generally. More than we all did. In that arts-studenty way. The way you knew how to think about things that everybody more normal would dismiss as a bit off the planet.

Normal.

Thanks, I said. I think.

I mean I know I was an arts student then too, she said. Of sorts. But never like you. I did it for the milk round, the jobs market. Not that I didn't or don't appreciate things. But I was never like you. Nobody else was. You were, well, different.

Was I? I said.

And I was lying there in the middle of the night staring at the curtains and you came into my head and I thought, Sand. I'll find a number or an email and ask Sand. Someone like Sand'll know what it means.

And here someone like me is, I said.

So. What do you think? she said. What does it mean?

Which part of the experience in particular? I said.

Just the words, she said. I'm not interested in anything but the words.

Curfew or curlew, I said.

Other way round, she said.

Curlew or curfew, I said

Curlew or curfew. You choose, she said.

Well, I said. That's the key. There's a choice. And it's something to do with *time* versus *bird*. I mean between the notion or actuality of time and the notion or actuality of a bird. A curlew is a bird, and a curfew is a time of day after which people officially aren't, by authority, permitted to be out and about. By law they're supposed to be home.

Yeah but that's obvious, I know all that, she said.

So the choice, I said. If there's such a thing as a real choice between the concepts evoked by two random words whose spellings suggest they've been yoked together like – or maybe even for – a kind of joke, maybe simply because they're almost the same word save for a single consonant change that minimally but effortlessly changes the meaning of everything –

Consonant change, she said. Oh. Oh yes. See, I never even thought of *that*.

– the choice, I said, is something to do with difference and sameness. And it's something to do with the dissonance between the words' meanings –

(I could hear her writing things down at the other end of the phone)

– *and* any similarity you can find between
the things the words stand for. For instance,
say, birds having wings and time being supposed
to fly –

Yes! she said. That's brilliant. You're such a clever
clogs.

– and if we think for a minute, I said, about the
short span but the apparent freedom in the life of
a bird, juxtaposed with the notion that what we
do with our allotted time can be, or arguably
always is, dictated or controlled one way or
another not by nature alone but by outside forces
like economics, history, social constraint, social
convention, personal psychology and political and
cultural zeitgeist. And if we think about the
proffered choice, curlew or curfew, between nature
and an authoritarian shaping of time, which is a
human invention, or between the environment and
our control of or harmful and expedient use of
the environment –

At the other end of the phone she started
laughing.

Expedient. Juxtaposed. Zeitgeist. Difference.
Dissonance. Consonant change, she said.

Uh, I said.

Tell you what hasn't changed, Sand, she said.
You. You haven't changed a bit.

I felt myself blush with no idea why I'd be
blushing.

Oh I don't know, I said. Definitely shifted a consonant or two of my own over the years, here or there.

Still the same old Shifting Sand, she said.

Shifting Sand.

Nobody'd called me that in years.

Well, nobody'd called me it full stop, at least never to my face. Not till this phonecall. Though I suppose calling me it on a phone – even on a kind of phone we could, should we want to, see people's faces on, a kind that was still imaginary back then when people called me it behind my back – still wasn't really calling me it to my face.

I mean, I knew that they called me it.

I assumed they did because I went out with people of both genders. That was seen as deeply dodgy, then, though not quite as dodgy as just being gay which is what I probably was / am and eventually as the time passed felt more able and determined to say.

Different times.

Anyway, now I was wide awake wondering whether Martina Inglis, about whom I'd not thought once in three decades, was happily asleep right now whoever and wherever she was in the world and wondering how on earth she'd known to make up the kind of story that really did intrigue even a deflated version of me.

It was almost as if she'd targeted me with it. The passports. The blank officials. The inexplicable and uncalled-for detainment. The revelation of the artisan beauty. The disembodied voice in the locked room.

She couldn't have made up a story more likely to hook me.

But why?

For the sly triumph that comes from playing with a life?

Or maybe even to empty my bank account? Scams were rifer than ever now. Possibly it wasn't even 'Martina Inglis' who'd phoned me. Possibly someone, some scammy people who didn't know me from Adam, had phoned me up pretending to be someone from my past. All sorts of details about people's lives were readily there on the net. Possibly it was someone who knew about the hospital / my father etc and figured I'd be particularly vulnerable right now. Easy game. Millions of pounds had been stolen already from thousands of people in this country alone, from isolated people desperate to trust a voice on a phone.

But.

There was no pretending in her.

Nowadays the least inkling of performance, pretence, selfishness, and I was off like a butterfly sensing a net.

I turned over in the bed. Okay. What I could do was, I could look up the famous lock thing. I could google it and check:

1. if it existed at all, and
2. if it did, whether it had been abroad on a tour of, what was it, post-medieval stuff, and
3. which museum it was associated with, and
4. whether she was on that museum's staff.

That'd all be a kind of proof.

But let's face it, Google itself wasn't exactly true. Everything onscreen and online was just the latest manifestation of realer-than-thou while being completely virtual therefore not in any real way real life.

And why the fuck, I thought punching the pillow in the dark, was I having to care about or think philosophically and existentially in the middle of the night about – think *at all* about – something that may or may not have happened in the head or in the life of someone I hardly knew and didn't even like that much, in fact consciously disliked, when I did know her?

I threw the covers off. I sat up.

My father's dog, across the other side of the room, sat up too, because I did.

Then she lay back down again when she realized what had woken her was only me.

Dogs were generally meant to be company. Companionable.

Companion able.

I'd heard the stories of people who, when isolated or imprisoned or lonely or suchlike, had found companionship in all sorts of unexpected places or things.

A small stone in the pocket.

A fragment of bone sewn inside a tiny leather pouch, bone said to have once been inside the body of a saint, passed down and down from parent to child to parent to child and clutched in the hand at every school exam or testing or troubled time in the life till it got passed down to the next generation to do the same thing with it. That kind of ritual thing, still meaningful even if it was nothing but a bit of a bone of a chicken sold as a piece of saint by a mountebank to someone who really needed a piece of a saint or thought it'd be useful.

Yes. A belief.

A belief was no doubt a companionable thing.

Sometimes just a tune. A song.

The words of a song.

The words of anything, a remembered line, even only half-remembered.

I'd heard the stories of people incarcerated, people in hostage situations, whose memories or minds, as they sat there in the fear and nothingness of whatever their situations were, literally opened like books and gave back so many things they thought they'd forgotten or didn't know they'd known, like they themselves *were* all the books they'd read and all the things they'd learned and done in their lives.

Books.

People said books were very companionable things.

Much like dogs were said to be companionable.

In the old days I had believed, too, that all of these things might well be companionable.

Alexas. People often said their devices were

comforting, like sort-of friends, maybe like those palm sized Japanese games all the kids had twenty years ago where you had to press buttons when the devices beeped to tell you they were 'hungry', because pressing buttons 'fed' them, and if you didn't press the buttons on time the 'life' in the device 'died'.

Radio.

People always said radio was very companionable.

I had my father's radio.

Sometimes in the middle of the night or the early hours of the morning I switched it on.

I'd gathered that programmes existed where, say, someone with a mic stood at the edge of a Venetian canal and just recorded the sound of the lapping of the water and then someone made a programme where nothing happened except that sound of water lapping in Venice. I'd have liked to find myself listening to something like that and I know I could easily have opened a laptop or used my phone to search then download or catch up on the likes of it. But there was something important, something that was the whole point, in the thought that I might chance to be listening to such a thing at the same time as random other people connected by real radioplay time were doing it too.

Instead, when I switched the radio on in the middle of the night over the course of this year, the kind of thing I encountered was news story after news story featuring government spokespeople telling me, much like they were reciting advertising copy, how this country was number one, first in the world, listing the things it was first in the world at and telling me how the thousand or so people still dying in this country every week was something we had to just chum along with now and how generous our government was being to everybody in the country by paying out so much public money to government friends and donors, how patriotic by picking fights with other countries. I'd heard how Black people were terrorists for organizing themselves into a protest movement that demanded equality and an end to racism. I'd heard how environmental protesters were terrorists for organizing themselves into a movement that demanded we attend to the ruination of the planet. I'd heard, beneath the lines, beneath the lies, how new laws would be voted through parliament so that protests like these would be outlawed and protesters like these would be curtailed and jailed. I'd heard how more new laws were on their way to stop anyone who asked for refuge in this country from getting here or getting help and to stop Gypsy, Roma and Traveller people from being able to live their ancient and traditional ways of life. I'd heard how the ancient rivers running through the country were filling with completely legal excrement

(I knew how dangerous this was already because one of my recent temp jobs had been in admin in the office of a water conglomerate and since our country had picked fights with the bloc where the treatment chemicals for sewage farms were made the conglomerates had been unable to source them and had been left with a surplus of untreated shit. I also knew that the virus loved to leave traces of itself in shit). I'd heard that the official advice for women who'd been stopped by, say, a member of the police force they sensed might want to coerce, attack, hurt, abuse and murder them was for them to try to *flag down a passing bus to ask for help.* I'd heard how some refugees who'd arrived in this country God knew how against all the odds were now being housed in the real cells of an old decrepit prison that had been being used till then as a sort of visit-a-prison theme park. I'd heard how inept and how callous this government was in abandoning thousands of people in Afghanistan now in danger for their lives because for the years of our presence in their country they'd worked with us.

I'd heard all this. Then I'd listened to a cabinet minister declaring that TV and radio etc should feature only programmes that celebrated *distinctly British values.*

PURE move. These were the words printed on the front of my father's radio, *move* presumably because you could easily carry it around while you went from room to room, *PURE* because of the persuasive lying crap that product branding generally is.

But anyway. I was past caring.

Here's the exact moment I passed it:

I'd spent the afternoon at the hospital. I'd come home to my rented space. I'd switched the kettle on. I'd switched the TV on. I did these things because I always did them. I didn't even notice myself do them; there wasn't much in my head that day beyond the lit windows of a high building I couldn't get into, my father up there in one of those squares of light.

A commercial for a fresh food delivery service came on TV. It was a vision of nourishment in which all sorts of bright colourful fruits and vegetables burst explosively out of cornucopic delivery boxes and families looked delighted as they did.

I stopped to watch it because the soundtrack to these fruitful images was a pop song I knew from years ago. It was a satirical song about the American aircraft that had dropped the first atomic bomb on the city of Hiroshima in Japan in 1945 which directly killed between seventy thousand and one hundred and twenty thousand people and injured another seventy thousand people.

POW! as they say in the cartoons.

What a lifestyle thing life has become, I thought. We used to march in protests. We had nightmares about our eyes melting in their sockets. Now a whole new kind of communal melting of the eyes was happening in front of mine, on primetime TV, and I'd understood fully, as I stood and watched it with my mouth open, why no government was ever going to give a fuck about and no history was ever going to think it worth recording never mind bowing its head even momentarily to the deaths and fragilities of any of the millions and millions and millions of individual people, with their detailed generic joyful elegiac fruitful wasted nourishing undernourished common individual lives, who were suffering or dying right now or had died over the past year and a half in what was after all just the latest plague and whose gone souls swirled invisible in shifting murmurations above every everyday day that we wandered around in, below these figurations, full of what we imagined was purpose.

What is there to say to that loss?

Everything becomes trivial next to it.

I sat in front of the TV watching the happy faces of the adverts.

A string inside my chest snapped, much as if I was a small stringed instrument tuned too tight.

Ow! as they say in the cartoons.

But then it stopped hurting and after that

nothing did and I no longer cared what season or what day.

As to my father. I'd boarded up the broken window. I'd taken the dog. I went regularly to the house and picked up the mail and checked there were no leaks, that the roof was okay and the heating still worked.

I had his radio.

I had his hat and his coat.

I had a few of his books.

I had his bank card. I found it on the bedside table the first time I got back from the hospital, it had a note crushed round it and his pin number scrawled on the note with the words *if I die take out as much as you can for as long as you can before you tell them Im dead youll need it*.

I had his watch, which was still going, at least the last time I'd looked at it, and had the shape and the sweat-darkened mark, the scent of his wrist, in the leather in the inside strap.

I had his glasses in his wornout glasses case with his name and the address of the house he lived in two houses ago written inside it in pen in his neat hand.

I had his old dog.

My taciturn father.

His taciturn dog.

Black labrador, ageing now, arthritic in the hips. She spent most of her time now she lived with me standing stiffly on the paving slabs of the back yard staring at nothing or sitting stiffly in the back room with her back to me staring out through the patio door at the same nothing in the yard. She slept in my bedroom on her blanket under the radiator because if I left her in the kitchen she whined all night. She ate what I put down for her twice a day. She asked to go out then asked to come back in then asked to go out, and so on.

What I knew about this dog was that an arthritic old dog knew more about my father than I did.

What this dog knew about me was that I wasn't my father and that I had a tendency to wake in the middle of the night and act as if there was an emergency happening somewhere that I had to get to.

Still.

Think about it, Sand.

Turnup for the books.

Tonight I'm not choking myself awake in a blind panic like I usually am at this time of night.

No.

Something about the story of that old lock mechanism had unlocked something in me:

knock knock.

Who's there? I say.

I say it like it's a joke.

The door opens. It's someone I vaguely recognize as one of the students in my class who hang out with the annoying and rowdy and arrogant group in the rugby club and the territorial army.

My own group of friends is made up of the people who the rugby club etc group call arty, who put on plays at the student theatre about the holocaust and gay people and nuclear missile silos and write short fiction and poems and publish these a couple of times a year in little pamphlets and who go to films with subtitles at the art gallery on Wednesday nights where the group this person who's at the door of my room hangs out with wouldn't be seen dead.

We drink at very different pubs.

Though we're often in the same rooms our paths almost never cross.

Hello, I say.

Yeah, hi, she says. It's Sand, isn't it?

She comes in and sits on my bed.

Eh, come in, I say.

I already did, she says and looks at me like I've said something really confusing.

I laugh.

Silence.

Want a coffee? I say.

No thanks. I just need your help with something, she says.

With what? I say.

I'm in your class, she says. I'm Martina Inglis.

Yeah I know, I say.

I'm in the other practical criticism seminar from you, she says. I'm supposed to be doing the poetry presentation paper this week for my seminar. I know you're doing the same paper, I mean the same poem, for your seminar.

Are you okay? I say.

She seems close to tears.

No, she says.

She tells me she wants me to give the paper I'll be writing about the poem we've been set to *her* so *she* can read it at the seminar she's meant to be writing this paper for too.

Yeah, that'll be right, I say.

You will? she says.

No. I was being ironic. Why would I do that? I say.

Last night, she says, I couldn't sleep. I thought I might go and jump off the Farr bridge. Then I wouldn't have to do any of this.

Uh huh, I say. But regardless of your impending nervous breakdown. If I give what I write to you and then I read out that same paper at my seminar, which takes place the day after *your* seminar, they'll think I copied it off *you*.

I keep thinking I'll throw myself out of the window of my room, she says. I keep imagining myself falling through the air.

You live on the ground floor, I say.

It's still got quite a drop, she says.

I laugh. She laughs too, though this makes her look even more likely to burst into tears.

I hate poetry, she says.

Then why are you doing an English degree? I say.

She shrugs.

I thought it'd be easy, she says.

It's as easy as you make it, I say.

It's not. And it's pointless, she says.

This poem's not even a big deal, I say. It's an e.e. cummings poem. You can easily write something about e.e. cummings. Anyone can say pretty much anything they like about e.e. cummings and it'll probably be a bit true.

I can't! she says. I've read it fifty times and I have no idea, not the fucking first fucking inkling, what it's fucking meant to fucking fucking mean.

She starts crying.

I find the duplicate the poem's on, bright purple from the copier, in among the stuff all over the floor. I come and sit next to her on the bed.

Okay, I say. Move fucking up. Here we fucking go.

Don't make fun of me, she says.

I'd never make fun of someone I don't know, I say.

I put the piece of paper with the poem on it down on the bed between us.

to start,to hesitate;to stop
(kneeling in doubt:while all
skies fall)and then to slowly trust
T upon H,and smile

could anything be pleasanter
(some big dark little day
which seems a lifetime at the least)
except to add an A?

henceforth he feels his pride involved
(this i who's also you)
and nothing less than excellent
E will exactly do

next(our great problem nearly solved)
we dare adorn the whole
with a distinct grandiloquent
deep D;while all skies fall

at last perfection,now and here
—but look:not sunlight?yes!
and(plunging rapturously up)
we spill our masterpiece

See? she says. *Nothing* about it means *anything*. I hate it.

Don't be hating a poem, I say. Waste of a strong emotion. Just look at the words. They'll tell you what they mean. Because that's what words do.

What? she says.

They mean, I say.

Yeah but what *I* mean is, why does he have to make it look so strange with all the spacing stuff he does? she says. It's like he's showing off.

Nothing wrong with showing off, I say.

Now, there I actually agree with you, she says. Though thousands wouldn't.

And it only looks strange because we expect spaces round punctuation, I say, and we expect punctuation and syntax to do very expected things. But why do we? Why do we have conventions at all?

Because how would we live properly without –, she says.

No, I don't need an answer to the question, I say.

Oh, she says.

I'm just highlighting one of the questions the poem's speaker's asking, I say.

The poem's speaker, she says. You mean the poet. Or is there another person meant to be speaking too? *God.* I don't understand *anything.*

I mean the person who's there inside your head when you read the poem, when the human thing you can hear through its strangeness, and the meanings you do recognize, even through the fog of the strangeness, all hit your eye and your mind, I say.

What? she says.

She looks at me, desperate, teary.

And here, I say. The poem, here it says *i who's also you.* So it's also about you, this poem.

Me? she says.

Whoever the me is who's reading it, I say. Me as well.

I just don't get it, from the start onwards, she says. What does it even mean, the first line? About starting and then hesitating and then stopping?

It means pretty much what you've just been telling me yourself, I say. That something about it, on the page, has made you look again, have to hesitate, even stop.

That's true, she says. That's true. But why *kneeling in doubt*? And all the stuff about skies falling?

40

Well you're the one talking about jumping off a bridge and out a window. Because you're so worried that you don't understand something. It's quite like your own sky has fallen in, I say.

Her eyes widen.

Oh, she says.

She wipes her nose.

But what about the kneeling? she says. Who's kneeling in doubt? Why?

Well, I say, something's definitely happening about doubt in the poem, and about collapse, and possibly about powers that are sky-high, I mean higher than human, powers that might require a person to pray, maybe. And it also suggests there's maybe a way to *stop* kneeling in doubt, maybe a way to be surer. At least that's the inference.

Inference, she says.

Look at what's beyond all the skies falling stuff, I say.

I point at the end of the third line.

Slowly trust, she says.

Doubt, followed by trust, I say.

Is that why the doubt and the sky falling are in brackets? she says.

I don't know. Could well be, I say.

And why is it in brackets in *one* part of the poem and *not* in brackets when it gets said again later near the end? she says.

Brackets mean containment, I say. Something set

apart, extra, maybe not necessary. The poet must want the sky falling first to be contained and then to be let loose, be something that becomes more salient as the poem goes on.

What's salient mean? she says.

It means salient, I say.

She laughs.

Good.

But what's that slowly trusting thing about? she says.

Hmm, I say. Something about giving over control? Something happening in the poem being a learning process in itself?

And yeah, okay, but what if what we're meant to be trusting is just, like, a list of random letters like the ones in the poem? she says. Where's the trust or the learning in that?

Yes, I say. But. All written words. Everything we make meaning with when we use written language. It's *all* just random letters, no?

Her eyes go wide.

Yes! she says.

I look at the poem again on the page. It does deal in what looks like a random fall of letters. They fall loosely through the poem all the way to the second last verse.

Maybe the poem wants us to trust meaninglessness, or something that doesn't mean anything, she says.

Yep. Possibly. But it's also asking us to trust the fall, if not of the sky, of the letters T and H, and then A, E and D, I say.

A and E, I know what that is, she says.

That's where you'd have been right now if you'd jumped off that bridge, I say.

Yeah, and D's what I'm going to get for this paper, she says. Thaed. *Thaed*. It's not even a word.

Unless, I say. Anagram. Sort of. Spell it sort of backwards.

Oh! she says. It's – death! is it? – it's death!

I smile. She smiles back, a broad, open-mouthed amazement of a smile.

How did you even *see* that? she says.

I didn't, till now, I say. Till I looked at it with you. And you're smiling at death now. Look how powerful a poem is.

Wow, she says. It's brilliant. But death in reverse. What does it mean? Are we supposed to be, like, trusting *death*? she says.

I suppose, I say. But not death per se. Death reversed, like you say. A death that's different from the usual death.

Look at you, she says, like that busker outside Marks and Spencer and all the meanings of things showering down round you like loose change.

The fall of meaning, I say. The fall of understanding. And here, look at the end. Where it says that there's even a perfection possible in what

43

we make of our own coming apart, well, that word perfection can mean a kind of end, or death in itself. But with this dissolution there's also, look, this surprise. Sunlight.

She shakes her head.

And then the word yes, I say. With its exclamation mark.

All this positivity. In death? she says.

In death backwards, I say. Death in reverse, to quote you.

Thaed, she says. He's playing a game with us.

A game with big stakes, I say.

I write H T A E D down on the paper next to the poem.

And I reckon he gives us the T and the H the right way round at the start to help with the game, I say. Otherwise the eye might be tempted to make the word into *hated* instead of the word death.

Yeah. Like I hate this poem, she says.

Do you still hate it? I say.

But she doesn't hear me; she's holding the paper with the poem on it and turning it round in her hands.

He's saying death's a game, she says. Which it really isn't.

Or saying there's a way to be playful even in times of really terrible doubt? I say.

Ah, she says. I like that.

Even when the day is dark and the sky is falling

44

and things and words and everything they mean are falling to pieces all around you.

Falling to pieces, she says. Way to be playful.

She reaches across and takes a pen off my desk and writes on the back of her hand.

PLAYFUL   DOUBT   PIECES

And at the end of this process, look, I say.

I point to the last bit of the poem.

Sun, she says. Up.

Dawn. That whole process of falling isn't a fall after all, it's a, a, I don't know, a rising up. An ascension.

Yes, she says. Like, is this a really religious poem?

You could make the case for that reading, yes, I reckon, I say.

Could I? she says.

She looks pleased.

Thanks, I say. I'd never have seen these thoughts in it unless we'd had this conversation.

She stands up.

They told me you'd be whizz-kid clever, she says.

They who? I say.

They also warned me not to come and ask you in case you made a pass at me, she says.

No worries. I only sleep with people I find attractive and who find me attractive back, I say.

But you're really good at this stuff, she says. It's actually almost cool. Even though it's so uncool.

Thanks again, I say.

I hate to say it, but we're quite good together, she says.

I wouldn't go that far, I say.

I feel so much better now, she says. How is that even possible?

The thinking game, I say. There's always a payoff one way or another.

So, she says. Now that we're friends. When you write it all down. Can I have a copy?

Nope, I say.

No? she says. Even though you said you'd never have seen those things in it unless you'd been talking to me?

Write down what you remember when you get back to your room, I say. Make up the rest. I guarantee our papers will be completely different. And we've only skated the surface of that poem.

A poem, like an icerink, she says. You write poems and things, don't you? You could write me a poem like an icerink.

Why would I do that? I say.

Did you know I'm quite a good figure skater? she says. I've medals for it.

Nope, I say.

You must be psychic, she says.

I look down at my watch on my wrist so that she'll know I want her to go.

You'll be fine, I say. Anyone could choose a single

phrase of this poem and write fifteen different papers about it.

At that she forgets her figure-skater self and looks cowed again, looks away.

I won't remember anything we said, she says. I won't be able to make it up.

Be playful, I say. You seem quite playful to me.

Do I? she says. Really?

Yes, I say. Now. Go away.

Be playful be playful be playful, she says to herself.

And don't jump off the bridge, this week anyway, I say. Only jump off it after you've asked someone else to help you with a paper for something else.

One day I'll help you with something, she says.

Sure you will, I say.

Don't tell anyone I was here, she says.

Your secret's safe with me, I say. So long as you don't tell anyone what everybody says about me behind my back.

Deal, she says.

Bye, I say.

Bye, she says.

She closes the door behind her.

All the years later, in bed watching the spring light come up round the light fitting in the ceiling of my rented bedroom, all I could remember, when I tried, of that time, was:

that once a long time ago I'd helped the virtual stranger who'd phoned me earlier that day analyse a poem we'd both been set as an exercise at college,

that the stranger had been freaking out about not being able to understand it,

that it was a poem by the American writer e.e. cummings. I'd liked him back then.

Now, though, I knew he'd supported McCarthy and the US witch-hunts.

Now it was clear, too, that he was also a penner of a scatter of outright sexist and racist little verses in there with all the luminous and sensually disruptive love poems and all the recalibrations of words, punctuation, grammar, possibility, meaning.

Sigh.

That was life. Everything suspect. Nothing uncorrupt.

Which of the poems was it, again, they'd set us back then for that exercise?

It had something like the letters of the word death falling through it.

Death in reverse.

All I remembered about Martina Inglis was that after that visit she'd made to my room to brainpick me we'd not exchanged a single word again, not once, the whole rest of the time we were at college.

I'd occasionally seen her in the distance, across a lecture room, in the refectory, walking past in the library.

When I did, if she saw me, she ignored me.

Fine by me. I ignored her right back.

But now, so far in the future, I felt better than I'd felt for a while. For half an hour at least I'd been not-thinking about how much I didn't care about anything.

Instead I was thinking of the turn in an ordinary stairwell in a library and how the window above it let light fall on it.

I was thinking of a day, a sunny afternoon when I'd been a student and I'd driven out of the city to an old ruined castle which nobody else ever seemed to visit, not whenever I visited it anyway. It had no attendant. It was just several stone walls and staircases with no roof, surrounded in lawn. Its insides were also all lawn.

Usually when I went there I went with friends. That day I'd gone alone. I'd climbed its spiral stone steps all the way up to its top and found a sunspot in the sheltered corner of one of its open walls.

Look, that's me, sitting on stone thirty feet up in the air, my back against more stone, reading a novel for pleasure, it's called Loitering with Intent, in the ruins of some long-gone rich person's castle, someone who would never have imagined possible a day that the roof would be off his house – definitely *his* house rather than *her* house here given history's predilections – and never have dreamed that one day the sun would hit this stony corner so uninterruptedly let alone that someone who, given history's predilections, would in other times have been skivvying up and down the stairs, would be sitting in it that sunny day reading a book for pleasure.

The ghost of a past possible me runs down the stairs at five in the cold morning to clean a fireplace and prepare a fire before the master gets up.

The ghost of a future-past me sits against the stone wall, with the book open and a view beyond it across the countryside for miles.

Here in the future-future, shortly I'd fall asleep.

I'd sleep properly and deeply that night with no difficulties. I'd dream a great dream, the kind dreamers recognize as a dream so good that they instruct themselves, even though they know they're asleep and dreaming, that they've to be sure to remember this dream when they're awake again.

In it I'd be wearing a kind of wolfskin over my whole self, the wolf's head on my head so that if I'd looked in a mirror I'd have had two heads, one on top of the other. But the wolfskin, I'd realize in the dream, wasn't an empty skin. It was a living wolf which had draped itself round my shoulders, not at all heavy, but warm, relaxed, as if happily hitching a ride.

I'd know when I woke up that I hadn't travelled with a wolf in any form since before my mother died. That's a long time.

Hello wolf, I'd say in the dream. Where've you been, old friend?

Look at its wolf-eyes exchanging a look in the mirror with me, its inner sheep.

Death in reverse:

they eventually wheel my father off the corridor and into a side room. It says STOREROOM on the door and it still is a storeroom but now it's also full of machines under its shelves of things and my father hooked up to the machines.

What I can see of the junior medic's face is grey with tiredness and yet she's still kind, takes her time with me, stands away from me but with me, at the entrance to the ward beyond which I can see my father in the bed through the door of the old storeroom, I can see the angle of his head, I can see the oxygen thing over his face.

The porter who helped us into the building and found us a holding space with the people on the trolleys told me that someone *just gone* had just been moved out of this storeroom and that this is our luck.

The medic tells me a lot of things. Then she says,

You can't stay. I'm sorry. We'll keep you informed.

Will it be okay? I ask her.

She looks straight at me.

Touch and go, she says.

Then she asks me to forgive her and excuse her. She turns to what needs her next.

I realize she seems to be wearing a binbag.

Someone else comes to the door and asks me to leave. This person is also wearing a binbag.

Are there still shortages? I say.

When weren't there? she says.

We'll phone you, someone else wearing a binbag says.

I put my hands in my pockets but I have no idea what I've done with the car key.

The junior medic on her way elsewhere must've sensed my panic. She calls across the corridor.

Does your car need a key in the ignition to start it? I bet when you go back to it and check the ignition you'll find the key still in it.

She is right. When I trace the car back to where I left it slewed half in and half out of one of the parking spaces, its engine is still running and one of the back doors still wide open like someone's just got out of it.

I close the open door. I get in the front. I reverse

out, pull the car in properly to the space, park it
properly.

I switch the car off. I sit for a moment.

I start the car again.

I have no idea where to go.

*

Twelve hours earlier.

While we're waiting between one thing and
another, by which I mean between the thing that's
just happened to his heart and the thing that's
about to, for the ambulance that's not going to be
able to come because there aren't enough
ambulances because so many other people are still
such urgent emergencies too, my father looks at the
blanket I've covered his legs with, pushes it off him
like it's burning him and before I can stop him has
rolled himself out of the armchair on to the floor
and is trying to lever himself up against the bedside
table and I am shouting.

He says he has to take the dog for a walk,
always takes the dog for a walk at this time of day,
imperative that he take the dog for a walk right now.

You don't, dad, I say, it's half past four in the
morning now, look, still dark, you don't take the
dog this early.

He slumps into himself, lets go of the bedside
table, lets his whole self heap down on to the rug
again.

Then he flails with one arm behind his back and brings out a shoe from beneath the bed. He pushes half his bare foot into the shoe. He isn't able to get the rest of his foot in.

He's saying something.

A girl. A girl will be wandering, no, wondering. A girl who says hello to him and the dog, she passes him on a bicycle on his dogwalk on weekdays. It seems to matter to him that it's weekdays. Then he asks me what day it is today.

You can't, I say.

He shakes his head.

He says the word.

Companion.

Then he says,

Abble.

He tells me like it's urgent that one day she said hello as she went past and the next day he said it back and now they say hello on weekdays.

Jest, he says.

Jest? I say.

Gesture, he says.

Dad, I say. Don't be silly. You're not going anywhere.

Then he tells me I'm not to do the dishes that are in his sink downstairs in the kitchen because I never do them properly and they're never clean when I do them.

Then he stops speaking.

He sits leaning sideways on the floor with both his arms round the legs of the bedside table. The shoe sticks weirdly off the top of his foot.

I'm standing above him waving my arms in the air.

I am, as ever, useless.

*

Three hours earlier.

Half past one in the morning.

My phone buzzes. My father has sent me a text. It says:

Cant move

The last couple of times we've spoken on the phone he's been talking about downsizing. What for? I'd said. Your house is perfect.

Feel like a change, he said.

That's a bit vague, I said.

Nothing vague about it, he said. I'd like a fresh start.

In the middle of a pandemic and at the age of nearly eighty you want a fresh start, I said.

Houses are fetching a good price right now, he said. Houses with gardens.

You like your garden, I said.

I'd like a bigger garden, he said. And a smaller house.

At your age? I said.

What's your problem with me wanting to live my

life? he said. You who's always lived your own life so, so, –

I know he's thinking the word selfishly.

My problem is it'll be me who has to do the moving work, I said. Then the gardening work.

That'll be bloody likely, he says. Never done a real day's work in your life.

Moving's one of the five most stressful things anyone can do in a life, I say.

I'm asking nothing of *you*, he said. I wish I'd never said a bloody word.

He hung up.

Now I look at the words on my phonescreen. Cant move. Good. He's come to his senses. But he usually goes to bed at ten. So he's clearly up in the middle of the night still stressing about the idea of moving.

I text back.

You so don't have to. It's your house you own it & v nice where you are.

He replies.

No cant move like a snake tight round my chest cant breathe

Ah.

Oh God.

Okay.

I phone the emergency service. They tell me there's an ambulance delay.

I'm not supposed to but I shoulder my clothes

on. I get in the car and drive there. I leave the car in the loading bay along from his house and I stand outside the front. His house is in darkness. The dog hears me, barks a couple of times.

I text my father and tell him I'm here.

He replies.

Dont come in might be virus

I send one back.

I'm coming in

He replies.

Chain on door

I reply.

I'll go round the back & break the kitchen window

He replies.

Dearth of tradespeople to fix it dont be stupid

My father, in the middle of an emergency, more worried about glaziers and his house than himself.

I dig a half-brick out of the flowerbed in the front garden and go round and smash the kitchen window.

＊

Two years earlier.

My father is waiting for me on the path by a pile of cut-down trees in a clearing. It's his birthday. He is his old self, I mean as opposed to his young self. The smell of cut wood is in the air and the space all around the pile of logs is trampled to mud and littered with woodchips.

Work well done by somebody, he says patting the side of the highest log. This one's the age of me. I counted the, the. You know.

Rings, I say.

I bend down and pick up a piece of inner tree the size of my hand. It's so light-coloured and fresh-smelling that I hold it to my nose then put it in my pocket.

Chip off the old block, I say. Wonder what they'll end up making with these.

These'll make something, all right, he says.

Firewood, I say.

Far too good for firewood, he says. They'll be for construction.

Sleepers, I say. Beams.

No! he says as if I should know better. These are beech. Perishable. Best for indoors. Floors, joinery. Suchlike.

I remember I'm supposed to say nothing really, just walk along, agreeing.

Good stuff, that, he says.

I can never help wondering, I say anyway, whether trees in a wood freak out when someone cuts down their neighbouring trees right in front of them.

Don't talk rubbish, he says.

He looks round for the dog.

Come on, he says to the dog, not me. Let's go.

Too happy, happy tree, I say.

He ignores me.

I know he's thinking about the garden centre on the other side of the wood where we always go when we do this walk to have whatever soup they're serving that day. I expect him to say, any moment,

wonder if they'll do the yellow fish soup today.

But then as we follow the bend of the path this is what he says,

they don't have to bother with all that happiness rot, trees. They're just trees.

Then fifty yards further down the path he says,

no such thing as a happy tree.

It's from the poem, I say, by Keats, about just that, a tree in winter that doesn't have to miss its summer greenness because trees don't remember or regret anything, and that's precisely why they're happy, because they just keep on being trees, doing what trees do. Till, you know, someone cuts them down.

I wait a moment. Then I say,

The picture I painstakingly painted and gave you last Christmas. That's a visual representation of the Keats poem the line's from.

Silence.

Then he says,

all that learning, and all you've done with it is make a life's work of for Christ sake painting words on top of one another so nobody can even read them.

Thanks for the critique, I say.

How would anyone ever know those words were *in* that painting? he says. Or *any* words?

But they are, I say. They're all in there. That's a picture of a poem and of all the words in that poem.

Visual representation. Just a slab of green, he says.

Green's the only colour Keats directly draws attention to in that poem, even though it's a winter poem, I say. Green felicity.

Visual representation, he says. Why not just paint a tree if you're going to paint the words of a poem about a tree?

That'll be why you left that picture I gave you in the garage under the old sweatshirt, I say. And that sweatshirt'll be stuck to the oil paint now and the picture'll be ruined. You know that, don't you? Ruined.

I always thought, when you were growing up, that child, she'll change the bloody world. You had every chance. But you went your own way. You always went your own way.

You know, dad, I could've sold that painting of mine that I gave you several times over if I'd wanted and got several hundred pounds for it when I did, I say.

Have it back, he says. Have it back. Sell it. Get your money for it.

Yeah, and I can sell the sweatshirt alongside it as its companion piece, I say. We could go into business, you and me. I'll do the painting, you do the ruining and we'll both profit from it.

Business, he says. You. Don't make me laugh.

I do fine, dad, I say.

No motivation. No ambition.

Different motivation. Different ambition, I say.

We both know we're talking about me being what he still thinks, even in the 21st century world of new freedoms and tolerant understandings, is the wrong sexuality here.

The life you could've had, he says. But no. Part-time work. To fund your nonsense. Visual representations.

I like my life, I say. I've chosen it.

A life spent waiting for paint to dry so you can paint paint on top of more paint, he says. Selling one or if you're really lucky two a year.

Money's not my motivation, I say. It's a discipline.

Painting words someone else has written one on top of the other. What the bloody hell's the point of it?

The point is, I said, that the words are there whether you can read them or not.

Bloody stupid, he says.

Silence.

We walk on down the path in the grey-green of the spring.

Ten minutes of silence later,

your mother liked trees, he says.

Mm, I say.

My father likes my mother a lot more now than he did when she was alive.

She especially liked a row of poplar trees from a distance, he says.

Yes, I say. I remember.

She liked when they line a road like they do, he says.

Good to know, I say.

She liked a good tree, your mother, he says.

*

Three decades earlier.

My father is one of his younger selves. He is letting the younger me drive his van, him in the passenger seat, to the halls of residence in which I've been allotted a room for my first year at university in a city a hundred mile drive away. I passed my test six months ago. The first time I took the van out by myself I backed it into a Give Way sign and ruined the back bumper and the boot. He swore he'd never let me in the driver's seat again. Until now he hasn't.

When we've arrived, driven up the leafy path to

the halls car park, unloaded my cases and bags and
ferried them up the three flights to the perfectly
formed small room that'll be the start to my life
away from home, he'll stand in the doorway, look at
his watch and say,

right then. Come on. You can give me a lift to the
train station and if you manage that without any
damage to the van and your driving's as good as it
was all the way here, then –.

He'll hold out the van key towards me.

Yours for your years here, he'll say.

What?

You'll need a car, he says. To come home in.
Regularly. Well, I mean, whenever you want to or
need to, I don't mean you have to.

But dad, I say. You need the van. For work.

Time I got a new one, he'll say. Good excuse to.

No way, I'll say. You can't. We can't afford it.

I'm doing it, he'll say.

He'll throw the key so that I have to catch it.

Come on. Station, so I can catch the 4.15.

But back before any of this happens, when we're
still on the road and about halfway there, with me
driving and him sitting in the passenger seat with
his hand poised just above the handbrake, he says
without turning his head,

tell me something. Say something about, I don't
know. Anything. You know. That way you have.

What way? I say.

With words, he says.

Oh, I say.

My mind empties of every word. I watch the sun glancing itself off the back of the car ahead of us on the road. It hits my eyes in the glance. I shade them.

Tell me something about today, he says. Anything.

Uh, I say.

He turns the sound on the cassette player right down. Wings at the Speed of Sound. We've just heard the song that starts with the doorbell ringing and is about how a lot of people keep turning up at a door, people who sound local or are family plus some people who sound like they might be from history since one of the people at the door in the song is Martin Luther. The song repeatedly asks whoever's listening to it to open the door and let all the people in.

Imagine if all those people in that song did turn up at your door, I say. Imagine Martin Luther, I mean turning up.

Open the door quick before he uses it as a noticeboard, my father says.

Or maybe it means Martin Luther King, I say.

Definitely let *him* in, my father says. A brave good man in the world. No. Let them all in. Whoever. Always honour everyone who comes to your door.

What if you don't like them? I say. What if the people at the door are people who've come to beat you up or, I don't know, take your home, or get rid of you because you aren't the same religion or colour or sexuality or something? What if something about you's put you on someone's hate list?

Christ almighty, my father says.

He's quiet for a minute. Then he says this.

All the same. Invite them in. Put the kettle on. What else you going to do?

I roll my eyes.

So, I say. Ask how many sugars they take *then* present your face to be punched?

Why are you thinking someone's at your door because they want to punch you? he says. Your world's a better place than ours was, girl.

Ask them if they take milk in their tea. Not much Widerstand in that, I say.

Not much –? he says.

It's the German word for resistance, I say. I mean. Put the kettle on. Pff.

Even I can hear how prissy I'm being now.

But next to me he's gone respectful, impressed, which makes me feel even worse.

That's what I mean. You've language, he says. That's a power beyond any punching. And by putting a kettle on I mean polite. Welcoming whatever's happening, whatever's going on.

That's resistance too. Grace under pressure, grace under pressure, your mother said it all the time.

My father almost never mentions my mother. Now he's talking about how he wonders whether or not she ever heard the song Wings did about giving Ireland back to the Irish.

I don't know that song, I say.

You were only small. They banned it at the BBC. God knows why, sweet little song, it was hardly going to cause riots. I bet them banning it made her angry, wherever she was then. Wherever she is.

She's in Windsor, I say. You know she is. She's got somewhere to live. She's sorting herself out. She's got a job. She works in the curtain shop.

She'd be proud of you today, wherever she is, I know that, he says. If she knew. College. Unthinkable, for me or her, a life like yours.

Here came my mother now at my door not with two or three knocks like normal people but with one clean hard thump to the ribcage.

Let her in?

She'll be measuring curtain material right now, I say. She'll be stretching it as far as her two hands can go on stretched-out arms, and lining the length of it up against the measuring stick on the counter.

Will she now? he says.

It'll be really thick cotton material, I say, and its pattern will be flowery. And she'll really dislike the pinks and blues and greens and how subtle they're meant to be, how classy, and how muted in reality. And she'll be struggling to overcome the urge in her to take that bolt of material, point it away from herself like a battering ram and hurl it with all her spirit's integrity through the plate glass at the front of the shop.

My father huffs air through his nose.

Integrity, he says. I don't know about the word integrity and your mother.

But she won't do that. She'll be standing in the shop after the woman who's bought the curtains leaves, I say, the bell on the door has just finished sounding through the shop air, and you know what she's thinking of?

He snorts anger beside me.

You, I say. She's thinking of you.

Hm, he says.

She's wishing she could've been the kind of woman who goes to a shop and buys curtains to put up in a house, I say. For you.

We drive on.

Your mother, he says a minute or so later.

He shakes his head.

She was a wild one, he says. That's exactly what she'd do. Throw a bolt of curtain material at a curtain shop window and shatter it.

Good. Her spirit's intact, then. At least what I imagine of her spirit given that I hardly know the woman who's my mother.

I apologize to her in my head for taking liberties with that last image of her standing behind the counter in an empty shop wishing she was the kind of woman who'd be buying curtains to make a husband's life look more like it should.

But maybe it's true.

Maybe she does long to be someone completely other than we'd readily or rather imagine her. Also, it's the image of her doing just that that's freed him to talk admiringly about her determination to be herself.

Then it's just us in silence, just the noise of the van round and under us moving us along, till I turn the sound on the cassette player back up.

The song playing now in the van is the one called Beware My Love.

*

Half a century earlier.

My father is a building contractor. He is home because it is Sunday. Because there are no days off for builders he's doing calculations at the dinette table for a sizeable contract. The table is covered with unrolled blueprints. The unwashed dishes from some of the meals we had this week are underneath the blueprints. He's pinned the blueprint papers down at the corners to stop them from rolling up again using some of these dirty

plates and a couple of little piles of my books off
the shelf behind him.

I am seven.

Sizeable. Contract.

I mouth the words without saying them out
loud.

He notices. He says,
stop doing that thing with your mouth.

I take a book off the top of the pile on the corner
nearest to me and start reading it in the middle.
It's the one with Findhorn the unicorn on the cover.
I open it at the page where the writing turns in
front of your eyes into the shape of a horse.

He reaches over and takes the book out of my
hands and closes it. He rolls his blueprints back off
the bit of the table closest to me. He starts
explaining to me how engines work.

He does this by opening this book at the back
and with the pencil from behind his ear drawing on
its blank inside cover the shape of an elf-hat, or a
mountain, or a tent, or from my side of the table
what looks like a capital letter V. At the top point
he writes the word FUEL. Up one leg of the V he
writes the word HEAT. Down the other leg he
writes the word OXYGEN.

He points to the space inside the V.

Inside, because of this combining, that's
combustion, he says. The fuel heats up and burns.
In the burning, the keeping the heat going when

these three things meet, that's where the energy comes from that drives the machine or makes whatever you need the fuel for work. One thing changes another thing into something else, and the result is? Is?

Something different, I say.

Something I wish you had more of. Energy.

Uh huh, I say.

I am not sporty enough for my father. I am weedy and not growing fast enough and since he started putting the white powdered stuff that's supposed to make me grow into all my food I am eating even less.

So. Come on. Think of some fuels, he says. You're the one that's good with the words. Tell me some words for fuel.

You, I say.

What do you mean me? he says.

You're a fuel. An old fuel, I say.

What? he says.

He hits me over the head with a rolled-up blueprint, but not too hard.

Tell me, come on, he says. Tell me what petrol is.

Petrol is six shillings and eightpence a gallon, I say.

You what? he says.

At the garage with the yellow and blue sign that has the head with the wings on its hat, I say.

My father looks at me like he can't understand me. Then he starts laughing.

Six and eight a gallon at the National, he says. You're right! That's what petrol is!

I'm pleased. He only rarely laughs.

Tell me about the National, I say. When you were my age.

When I was small, a lot younger than you, he says, the National was still the forge, where they brought the town's horses to be shod. The town was much smaller then, and where the National is now was the very edge of it, and I used to like to sit on the wall and watch Mr Duncan the farrier, he was always telling me how the smithies were all being converted one after the other all over the country into petrol garages, for cars. Not long now, he'd always say. This place's not long for this world.

Tell me about you not sleeping and the horses, I say.

The horses, he says.

And your mother, I say.

I've told you a million times, he says.

Please, I say.

The faraway look comes into his eye. It always does when he's anywhere near the word mother.

One night I was awake when I should've been asleep, he says. I was sitting up in the bed, all my brothers were asleep round me but I was sitting upright, straight as a gate. And my mother came in, she said, what's the matter? Get down in that bed and off to sleep. And I told her I couldn't sleep,

I was worried one day there'd be no one left to put the shoes on any horses.

He looks at the pencil in his hands. He tucks the pencil behind his ear again.

Hay, I say.

Hey what? he says.

Old fuel, I say.

Don't call me that again Sandy, don't be impolite, or the back of my hand'll polite you.

No, I say. Hay. It *is* old fuel. Horsepower.

Horsepower? he says. Oh. *Hay*. Ha.

And dad, I say. What does straight as a gate mean?

Well, it means –, he said. Well, I don't exactly know what it means.

Is it a saying everybody says? I say. Or just you?

I don't know, he says. I've always said it. I suppose it means a gate's got to be put in straight, put in properly, or it'll fall down or not open properly.

I think you just say it, or people just say it, because it rhymes, I say.

And you're too clever for your own good, he says. What's petrol. Six and eight at the National.

After that, for quite a long time, whenever we hear the word national, if someone mentions the petrol station or someone on TV talks about the national anthem or national savings, national security, national costume, national treasure,

National Velvet, anything, my father will wink at
me and shout across the room,
    that's what national means, isn't it? A place you
pay through the teeth for something that makes
things, come on, makes them what?
    Combust, I say like I'm meant to say.

The day after that phonecall with the story about the historic lock happened to be my father's birthday. I'd struck a match in my front room. I'd lit a candle.

But when I did it was a bit like I was acting like I would if he were dead rather than just in a hospital I couldn't visit.

So I blew the candle out.

Only the day before I'd been past caring, though unequivocally not past despising myself. I'd got so used to both of these states that I was surprised to find myself thinking to light a candle, then surprised again when I could smell the match on the sandpaper then smell the blown-out candle and yet didn't despise myself because *I* could smell these things and my father *couldn't* smell these things.

75

Now, for a reason I couldn't fathom, I no longer despised anything.

I left the dog at home. I didn't want the responsibility. I drove out of town past the supermarkets and the flyover, out past the flower nursery where the unpicked daffodils were heaped-up dead and rancid on the verge of one of the flowerfields.

I parked the car where we always parked.

There were no other cars parked there.

I took the path we usually took.

There were no other people on the path.

There were no logs this year cut and waiting at the side of the path where the logs usually were. There was no sign there'd been anyone working in the woods and no point in me heading towards the garden centre; the garden centre'd gone out of business. I'd have given a lot to have my father yell at me over the garden centre rosebushes this year, us rowing as usual over row upon row of roses alphabetically arranged and waiting to bloom, The Ancient Mariner, Atomic Blonde, Beautiful Britain, Charles Darwin, Cliff Richard, Dame Judi Dench, Scepter'd Isle, Thomas à Becket. Maybe they were all still in there untended, wild-intertwined. Maybe the closed garden centre was a riot of life now.

In fact, there was no point, I thought as I walked the path we always took, in taking this path through the woods at all. Which is maybe why

I stepped off it – that, and the fact that I'd seen or thought I'd seen moving freely through the trees a deer? a small horse? did horses wander about by themselves in these woods? Unlikely. I followed what I thought I'd seen to see if I could see what it was.

Then I stopped. Any path was gone.

I turned a full circle on my heel.

Turning a circle made almost no difference. All round me were the same different slim tall trees leaning towards other slim tall trees, threshold after possible threshold made by the ways they bent towards and away from each other.

It had taken me thirty seconds to get completely lost.

It was as strange as I'd heard people say it is when someone goes into one of those rooms so soundproofed that all they can hear is their own heart, the blood going round their body, the movement of their own guts and saliva. Except, what I heard was what was there when we're not there to hear it. I heard trees creaking, not something I knew till then that trees in a wood did, like they were speaking a language to each other. Beneath that the sound of the wing movement of an invisible bird, the call of another then another and below me the noise that grasses make when they move. Yes, like a shift of sound, an apparent absence of sound becoming a new sound palette in itself.

People also chose, didn't they, to go into a room designed to cut them off completely from any light source so they could experience 'real' darkness. Why would you? When there was so much darkness in light itself, like the endless shifting moving ever-changing lights and darks right here.

Not for nothing so many folktales and fairy stories took place in woods.

For a short while somewhere foolish in me expected what would happen next to be something like:

and then I heard what sounded like people working somewhere off to the left of me so I turned towards them and when I found them they pointed me towards the path back,

or

but soon I could smell the scent that meant that someone not far from here had lit a fire so I followed the smoke and my nose and came across a clearing with people in it who live in the woods / work in the woods / were having a day out walking in the woods / were cooking something over the fire and offered me some and were extremely good company,

but none of this happened.

What really happened was, I was lost.

I was alone.

I couldn't hear the traffic noise from the motorway any more.

Dusk was falling.

I had no idea where I was or which direction to begin to take.

All there was was all there was.

I dropped down on my haunches in the new long grass and the old bramble tendrils. I unpicked a tiny thorn from my sleeve and reached to drop it away from me on the moss. Then I stopped. I held it up to my eyes and looked at it as closely as I could.

It was small enough on the tip of my finger to make the ridges in my fingerprint look quite large. It was black, tough so that when I pressed it between fingers there was no give in it at all. It had a little hook on its end and against the lighter colour of the tip of my index finger I could see this hook had a curve in it and a cunning way of doing what it was meant to do, dissuade by piercing and hooking under the surface of whatever would try advertently or inadvertently to devour, hurt or mess with whatever plant it had come off.

It looked a piece of perfect engineering.

I hooked it back into the place it had caught in my sleeve. It disappeared into the material.

I sat on a felled dead tree alive with ivy. Above me the trees were bright with the beginnings of their new green. A bird hurled across the piece of sky through the greenness, called beyond itself.

The trees spoke their language.
The light and dark took turns.
What I knew was my own absence.
What I sensed, clear as unruined air, was the
ghost of a chance, a different presence.

Curlew

Goodbye v hello:

I am four and a half years old. The daylight is coming through the glass panel in our front door behind her as my mother, who's about to run out on my father and me – like out of petrol, out of patience, like she's money or a membership, spent, expired – is hugging me against her legs in the hall. Then she comes down so her face is at my level, puts her hands on my shoulders and says,

you'll be fine. I'm not worried for you. Because, you know what? There is a dog, a big one, very thick fur, very like a wolf, in fact it's not a dog, it *is* a wolf, and it's sitting right next to you.

I look all round me but there's no dog or wolf.

You can't see it, she says. But I can.

Is it like the dogs the man who comes to get the rent brings with him? I say.

Even fiercer. And it's yours, nobody else's, it belongs to you and you to it. It will never leave you, and it means you well, she says.

There's no dog or wolf. There's nothing. But she is looking at me like she can see something.

Did any of this even happen? I'd no idea.

Did my father tell me it afterwards to make me feel better, make something more bearable for me? Or did I make it up to make myself – or even my father – feel better? More likely.

I knew hardly anything, only the things my father told me, and he'd told me hardly anything.

That she liked that poplar thing etc.

That she could be reduced to tears, to fury, by very sweet and simple piano melodies.

I liked this version of her. I liked to imagine that what infuriated her was the audacity of their sweet simplicity, that this somehow made her conscious of their silent companion, the complex cruelties that were always happening so very simply everywhere.

I imagined this precisely because of something else, the most vivid of all the things my father'd told me about her.

One day when my mother was a child in Ireland and one of her sisters was very ill, she was sent to fetch the doctor. She was eleven years old. On the way across the fields she met a young Traveller woman carrying a baby. The woman asked her for money.

The child who'd one day be my mother had no money. I mean no money at all. There was no money even to pay the doctor, just the hope that he'd maybe come. But he was a different religion from my mother's family and disliked them for all sorts of reasons including this difference, so nothing was certain.

The child my mother was apologized to the woman.

The woman took the child my mother's hand, turned it empty palm upward and looked at what was and what wasn't in it.

There'll be a death in your family at half past three, she said.

True?

I'd no idea.

True or false, my mother'd definitely had a sister who died. You could verify such things online.

She'd more than likely gone for help there was no surety she'd receive.

When she was older she'd told this story, of how she'd been met by a woman who told her the future honestly, and for no payment.

Story v lies:

knock knock.

My father's dog started barking like crazy.

Two clean-cut young people were standing on my doorstep. They were twins. Were they new neighbours? I didn't recognize them. Both had exactly the same haircuts styled fresh from a hairdresser recently reopened. Both were wearing matching smart light blue trouser suits. One had a bag that said the words CELINE Paris on it. The other's suit jacket was hanging open so that I could see, on the white T-shirt underneath, the words *they / them* handwritten on it in Sharpie.

Yes? I said.

Can you just get that dog to stop barking, I mean right now? the CELINE twin said.

Sure. She's only barking because you knocked on the door, I said.

The they twin said nothing. They glanced away down the road as if embarrassed, or as if at something much more important happening elsewhere.

I'll certainly see to it if I can that she barks less, I said. Thank you for letting me know.

I went to shut the door.

No, we're not here about your bloody dog, the CELINE twin said.

Oh. Right. How can I help you, then? I said.

We'd like a word, she said.

Which word would you like? I said.

We all three stood there in silence for some seconds until I realized they were waiting for me to invite them in.

Oh, I'm sorry, I said. I'm letting nobody inside the house. A member of my family is poorly and in hospital and I'm keen not to endanger him.

Covid's over, the CELINE twin said. The government says.

I realized she was a lot younger than I'd first thought.

Yeah but what's said about what's happening and what's really happening are often quite different things, I said.

We're not ill, the CELINE twin said.

It's not that easy to tell by looking, I said. Have you got masks?

Absolutely not, the CELINE twin said. We've nothing to hide.

Uh, I said. Excuse me for a moment.

I reached to the hallstand and got my own one.

Eye em oh you've a lot to answer for, the woman said.

What? I said.

You heard me, she said.

Yes, I did, I said. But I didn't understand the first thing you said there.

Eye em oh, she said again.

Uh. Right. What exactly is it you think I have to answer for? I said.

We want you to stop upsetting our mother, she said.

Then she told me they were the children of Mrs Pelf.

I shook my head. I didn't know anyone called Mrs –.

Ah, I said. Okay. Come through to the back of the house.

I opened the side door to the yard and stepped away as they went through. They sat on the bench by the back door. I went to the far end and sat crosslegged on the ground with my back against the studio door.

Because of you our mother's acting like a mad woman, the CELINE twin said.

Because of me, I said.

She's always got up at 6.50, all our lives. But now, nine or ten in the morning if she's not working. Our father can't function.

Oh dear, I said.

She won't listen to him. She won't listen to us. At night she goes off out in the car by herself and doesn't come back till all hours and won't tell anyone where she's been.

None of those things sounds all that mad to me, I said.

You don't know her, she said.

You're quite right. I don't, I said.

Does she come here in the evenings? she said.

Here? No, I said.

She's really different now. She stands around in the kitchen and the lounge laughing at nothing. The last time I left Amelie with her, that's my daughter, I came back and they were making a necklace out of a piece of string and the contents of a tin of spaghetti hoops.

I laughed out loud for the first time in weeks.

It's really not funny, the CELINE twin said. Clothes ruined, tomato stuff all through Amelie's hair. And she keeps telling Amelie really frightening stories and now Amelie isn't sleeping, she wakes up shouting about all sorts, birds with beaks as long as swords, horses with their legs cut off, eye em oh it's *grotesque*, it's really, really disruptive. And that's another thing that's changed. She never used to laugh at anything. Now she laughs all the time. Just like you just did. In the middle of people talking to her, even. And she keeps saying words. Out loud.

What, you mean speaking? I said.

No because it's not *to* anybody. She just *says words*. Words that aren't words we've ever heard her say.

What kind of words? I said.

She stands there going, *I'm amazed*, the CELINE twin said. Things like, *life is amazing*, and *who knew this could happen*, and then she just stands there smiling and shaking her head.

It sounds a little like she's in love, I said.

That's disgusting, the CELINE twin said. She's a nearly sixty-year-old woman.

Well, properly speaking she's fifty six.

The they twin had spoken at last.

And we know from someone at her work, someone with her best interests at heart, that she's been going into the digital records system and changing attribution and all manner of historical and necessary cataloguing information, the CELINE twin said.

How do you know it's her who's doing this? I said.

They've traced it back to her computer, the they twin said.

That doesn't mean it's your mother doing it, I said.

She's going to lose a prestigious part-time

position because she's acting so adolescently, the CELINE twin said holding her phone pointedly towards me.

Are you recording this? I said.

Why is your number in her phone and why are there several mentions of your name in the search history of her laptop? she said. You're having an affair with our mother.

No, I said.

Is our mother here in your house right now? the CELINE twin said still holding her phone at me.

I already told you. No, I said.

Is that why you won't let us into your house, because she's here and you're lying about it? she said.

I leaned forward and spoke at the phone.

Your mother's not in my house, I said.

Won't let us into the house so we've no way of knowing, the CELINE twin said into her phone.

Please explain to whoever's listening, I said, that I'm not likely to let a couple of strangers who might be scammers into my house.

We're not the scammers here, the CELINE twin said.

If she says she's not in her house, the they twin said, then she's probably not in her house. Come on, Eden. Let's go.

Then where *is* she? Eden Pelf said in a wail. Where else could she *be*?

So she's gone a-wandering, I said. Well well.

What are you smiling at? Eden Pelf shouted. She's a fucking missing person.

Eden. Don't, the they twin said.

That's different, I said. I'm sorry for being flippant. How long has she been missing? When did you last see her?

First thing this morning, Eden Pelf said.

It was only noon now. I couldn't not laugh.

You're obscene, Eden Pelf said. Laughing at our loss.

Eden, the they twin said.

They turned to me.

Are you having an affair with our mother?

I shook my head.

But you do know her, they said. She does know you. You've been in touch. Recently.

We know you have and we're going to the police, Eden Pelf said. We know the police. My father's very well known. We're friends with the authorities. We're friends with very powerful people. We'll take you to court. We'll go to the press. We'll get you vilified on social media. You'll be cancelled. You'll lose your job. We'll make sure everybody and everything boycotts you.

I shrugged.

It's *your* mother who got in touch with *me*, not the other way round. We've spoken only twice in more than a quarter of a century, and the first time

was when she phoned me one evening recently.
Then she sent me a zoom link and we spoke to each
other on that for just over half an hour. That's the
sum total of my dastardly hold on your mother.

What about all the texts you've been sending her?
Eden Pelf said.

What texts? I said. I didn't send any texts. Oh.
Wait. I did send one text.

One text! Eden Pelf said. Liar.

No, the they twin said. Truthfully, Ede, we did
only find one text on there.

Yeah because our mother'll have deleted the others
because they were incriminating, Eden Pelf said.

The they twin turned to me.

This text we did find. It says, and I quote, *I've
something for you*. What did you actually give our
mother?

Was it drugs? Eden Pelf said.

What are you both doing looking at your
mother's private personal devices? I said.

We're only trying to help our mother, the they
twin said. Please help us.

So I told them I'd told their mother a story.

And that's it, I said. That's all.

What, Eden Pelf said. Like, a *news* story?

A story, I said. A story story. She told me one, so
I told her one back. Fair exchange.

Like an old-fashioned once upon a time story?
the they twin said. Like a bedtime story?

You're a disgusting person, Eden Pelf said, playing a perverted game with a woman to seduce her away from her children.

Look, I said. Your mother got in touch out of the blue and asked me to respond to a few things in her life that felt mysterious, and what she told me took the shape of a story. So when we got back in touch I told her what had come to mind regarding that mystery, and it took the shape of a kind of story too.

Whoa. Quirky, the they twin said.

Manipulating our mother, Eden Pelf said. By telling lies.

No, I said. People who tell lies are only interested in the enslavement of their listeners to some cause of their own.

She's enslaved our mother, Eden Pelf said. She's in love with our mother and she's stalking our fam. She wants to break our fam into little pieces.

I'm not stalking anyone, I said. I don't even know where your mother, or any of you, lives.

Yeah but a story about what? the they twin said.

You'd best ask your mother that, I said. But I've a question for you. How come you know where *I* live?

We know all about you, Eden Pelf said. Lee works in eye tee at eye gee.

Is that your name? I said. Lee?

Yeah, the they twin said. Lea with an a. El ee ai. And this is Eden.

And what's eye gee? I said.

Boomer alert, Eden Pelf said.

Insta. But I don't work for them any more, I'm outsource now, I'm in data, Lea Pelf said.

I looked at Lea Pelf again, and then at the sharpied words *they / them* on their T-shirt.

You know, I've often thought, I said, that if given the chance, the tiniest verbal shift, like on your T-shirt, can make everything possible.

Told you, Eden Pelf said. Boomerissimissima.

Lea Pelf looked at me sharply for the first time and said,

are you taking the piss?

No, I said. It's one of this era's real revolutions. And one of the most exciting things about language, that grammar's as bendy as a live green branch on a tree. Because if words are alive to us then meaning's alive, and if grammar's alive then the connection in it, rather than the divisions in us, will be energizing everything, one way or another. It means an individual person can be both individual and plural at the same time. And I've always believed there's real room to move in embracing the indeterminate.

Actually I'm very determined, Lea Pelf said. And in my usage it's a singular they. It's to signal that gender is irrelevant to me. It's to cancel the binary.

Powerful little word, I said.

Yeah, you're right. So powerful, Lea Pelf said (and pointedly leaned to say it as close to the phone their sister was holding as they could), that my father's made me move all my stuff out of the house and into the garage.

Eden Pelf frowned and put her hand over the phone mic.

– and won't let me in the house till I *stop buggering about* and use what he calls the *traditionally correct pronoun* to refer to myself again, Lea Pelf said.

Ah, I said.

I leaned towards the phone again.

The word *they*, I said, has been used traditionally grammatically as a singular form since medieval times and for exactly what you're expressing when you use it.

Thanks for the gesture of support, it's nice of you. But I don't need you or anyone to make the case for me, Lea Pelf said.

Well, I said. It's been very nice to meet you both. Thank you both for coming.

I smiled with my own preconceptions on both Martina Inglis's / Pelf's children. They looked back at me with their grown faces full of their preconceptions about me. I stood up and opened my arms in that end-of-the-meeting way. They sat on the bench and didn't move.

We're going nowhere, Eden Pelf said, till you give

us your word never again to come near our mother. Or us.

You have my word, I said. Now you can go somewhere.

I went to the back gate. I stood by it, open. They still didn't move from the bench.

We're going nowhere till you tell us how to get our mother to go back to being the person she used to be, Eden Pelf said.

That's the kind of mystery you'll have to deal with yourselves, I said.

Come on, Ede, Lea Pelf said. We've done all we can here.

They pulled their sister to her feet and pushed her towards the gate.

We know where you live, Eden said as the gate swung shut behind her. We'll be back.

Bring masks the next time, I called after them.

Then I washed my hands and went into the studio again to get on with my work.

Imagination v reality:

I've something for you. I clicked the link on the screen. Martina Inglis, the same but different. Different but the same.

She was sitting with not just a table but tables behind her loaded with fruit and ceramics, and space, and was that a balcony above her? under a roof that went back for ever and was mostly glass.

Sands of time be damned, she was saying. You look exactly the same. After all these years. Have you sold your soul to the devil?

I've only half an hour or so, I said.

God, you *really* haven't changed, she said. Nice to see you too.

I got in touch because I've this tale to tell you about what happened to me the other day, I said.

98

Okay, she said. Great. Knew you would. Knew you wouldn't let me down. I'm all ears.

So I got home, I said, mid evening, just gone dark, I'd been for a walk in the woods, and I opened my front door and I could smell a kind of singeing smell, metallic, like someone had set something earthy like a lump of peat on fire somewhere in my house. I went through to the back then came to the foot of the stairs again. The smell was everywhere.

A lot of people are having weird olfactory sensations right now, she said.

Don't interrupt, I said, there isn't time. Let me tell you everything I can remember first and then we can talk for as long as I've left, I've to be at a hospital in an hour.

Are you ill? she said. You don't look ill. Who's ill?

So I went round downstairs putting all the lights on, I said, then I started to worry that maybe some electrical malfunction was happening in the walls so I went round putting all the lights off again. Then I went upstairs in the dark.

I opened my bedroom door.

There was someone in there, hunkered down behind the bed and rooting around in my wardrobe. I mean there's not much to steal in my wardrobe. I put the light on. It was this person in filthy ripped sort of clothes, clearly a homeless person or someone on drugs who'd broken into the house and all the shoes and boots I keep in the bottom of the wardrobe were out all over the floor and my father's dog was sitting on my bed where she knows she's really not allowed, and looking at me like it was *me* who was the intruder not the person going through my things.

And then I noticed there was another creature on the bed next to the dog, quite a large creature, size of a small turkey. Except it looked like it had no legs and no head.

Were you hallucinating? Martina Inglis said. A lot of people are having postviral hallucinations.

So I said to the dog, get off the bed this minute, you, and I said to the person, how did you get into my house? and she lifted herself off the floor out of the wardrobe and turned round and looked at me, it was just a girl, sixteen maybe, and her face and hands were smeared with dirt, her whole self looked like she'd been, I don't know, stealing coal from a slagheap in a British film from the 1960s, and I could see she was putting one of her really filthy bare feet into one of my best winter boots, and she looked straight at me while she did it, insolent, and she said, this dog needs a lot more than you're giving it, what kind of a beetlehead are you? I said, what are you, the dog police? and she said, new shoes. You have more shoes than your feet need, you won't miss them, and I said again, how did you get into my house? She said, easy, with a dumb. Just share me the shoes, and the bird and I will leave you to God,

and right then the headless thing on the bed unfolded a head out of itself, it *was* a bird, it had been tucked into itself, into its own feathers, and its beak as it untucked it was amazing, as long as, well, longer than any bird-beak I've ever seen or could have imagined existed, long and thin and as delicately curved as, I don't know, some very thin ceremonial sword, and it sat up next to my father's dog who was still there on the bed and its bird face with that beak was like it was wearing one of the plague masks you see in pictures of when people wore them in Venice back in the centuries, so that the length of the mask would keep the germs at a distance, and it looked straight at me with its deep black eyes.

Oh my God, Martina Inglis said on my screen. It's the curlew.

Eyes like little black lights, I said. Then it sort of struggled up, beat its wings, its wingspan was way too big for the room, it knocked the lampshade swinging, sort of leapt up in the air and settled itself on the shoulder of the girl, she squared her shoulder to take the weight of it and she turned to me.

Can I have them or not? she said. Do I have a choice? I said. Where are your own? On the feet of the loper who took them off my feet. When? I said.

When we were on the road, she said. You're in a band? I said. I mean she seemed quite young to be on the road in a band. But she nodded.

I was in the Brotherhood of the Company of the Craft, she said.

I racked my brain but I'd never heard of them.

What do they sing? I said. Anything they like, I'm not with them no more, she said, they threw me loose. Never mind, my tools are my own, now I'm journeying.

Some kind of groupie? She was way too young to be this homeless and druggy.

Nails, she was saying now, and spikes and all decoratives, I'm the fellow. What needs mended here? Not counting this poor dog you've broken. The break's an inner crack, yours to mend, I can't, but I'll trade you a piece of house goods that need mending for a sleep under a roof, I've a tolerable hand, stew pans, lock, grate, kettle, candlestick, hinge, last a lifetime, you've my word, I'm good at knives, there's many a person buried with a knife of mine for use in the next life.

She was high on something, God knew what. Either that or she'd learned her syntax off some old Poldark episode.

But the mention of a knife.

What's your name? I said. Won't if you don't mind, she said. Best not to. She put her hand in the air, ruffling the bird as she did, jerked her hand upwards and moved her head as if she was holding a noose and the noose had just broken her neck.

Dear God, I said. Don't be doing that.

So can I take these shoes or no? she said.

She'd managed to get her feet into my good boots and now she was marvelling at the zip fastener on one of them.

I told her she could have the boots provided she tell me who her parents were, where they lived, how I could find them so I could let them know she was okay, and a bit about her own story.

She said she'd tell me if I swore to give this poor dog its due. I told her I would. I told her she was quite right, it was astute of her, that I'd given the dog nothing she really needed apart from food and water. The girl nodded and the bird sitting on the back of her neck glinted at me with its beak curved round down past the girl's shoulders and chest like a festival sash or a line nobody was to cross.

She sat down on the carpet; the bird rose for a moment when she did and settled on her shoulder again.

Then she told me good luck to me trying to find her parents because they were well dead, and that her story was that she was good with horses. She told me she'd got thrown out for fornicating. Then she went off on one, a long deluded story about a holy man she'd got involved with, called Loy? or maybe Lloyd? who clearly worked in the same place as she did, and about how once he was called to put a shoe on a horse that had a sore leg that it wouldn't let anyone near, it bucked and kicked and had knocked three people cold already. So the holy man took a very sharp knife and sliced the whole of the sore leg off the horse, and the horse stood there calm on its other legs and watched as the holy man shod the hoof of the leg he'd cut off then stuck that leg back on to the horse's body and soldered it tight with a hot iron.

Oh he has the devil by the nose, Lloyd, she said. He can hold him far far off and keep him there with the length of his pincers,

and the bird on her neck opened its beak and closed it like its own beak could demonstrate how.

She told me all this with a kind of clarity I wouldn't have expected, or perhaps should only have expected, from someone so drugged out of their face on something or other.

The deal was, I said, that you were to tell me where your parents are and what your story is, and instead you've told me a lot of rubbish.

If I say it's my story, she said, who are you to say it's not my story? You want to help me, give me shoes. Give me somewhere to rest in the dark, man.

You can stay here as long as you like, I said.

I'll only stay as long as I need.

Would you maybe like to wash? I said. She asked me what month it was, and when I said April she said no, she washed in May. So I got her a blanket, took her downstairs, watched her cover herself with it on the sofa. She settled down. The bird settled on her chest with its head turned backwards and its beak tucked into itself again. My father's dog came down too. She lay on the floor next to the couch like she was with them, not me.

I sat on the other side of the room and waited till the visitor was asleep. When she was, I went online and typed in *music Brotherhood of Company of Craft*. But nothing came up, just some stuff about that old 70s band that won Eurovision and an American beer called Brotherhood. Then I thought how I could check to see if there were any photos of missing people online who looked like her.

I crossed the room to try to sneak a photo on my phone that I could forward to anyone who might be looking for her.

Below her neck there was this damage on the skin, a nasty-looking zigzag at the collarbone like an infected burn.

The bird with its backward head opened one black eye. The girl had one eye open and on me too.

What happened to your collarbone? I said.

A beauty, she said. Clean line, when it heals.

Delirious. Maybe it wasn't drugs. Maybe it was an infection off such a bad burn.

I've some Savlon in the bathroom, I said.

Salve on, she said. I can do healing too, I'm taught. I can cure a lady with the cooling water, and a child with the bandy legs with it too, and a hot iron does good to any wound especially an angry mouth in a horse, if you've a horse with an angry mouth.

I shook my head. I've no horse, I said.

She closed her eyes. Pity, she said.

The bird on her chest on the blanket closed its eye too.

I closed my eyes now onscreen to Martina Inglis, exactly as if I was saying the words the end.

I counted to five.

I opened them again.

Martina Inglis was sitting in the blank space looking back at her screen with me on it and she was as wide-eyed as a child.

And that's it. That's all. I said.

No. But something must have happened next, she said. What happened next?

I don't know. She'd gone by the time I got up, I said. The blanket left neat on the couch. The dog at the door looking mournful. She took the boots. She took the Savlon. I was glad she took the Savlon. Someone needs to have a look at that burn.

But the bird, the bird on her shoulder, she said. It's the curlew. Isn't it?

I don't know, I said. I've no idea. To be honest it looked like an impossibility. Such a long beak, how could any bird have one that long and not break it every time they tried to eat anything?

That girl in your house, she said. She's a personification. Isn't she?

No, I said. It was a person.

A vision, she said. Of the person who made the Boothby Lock. Isn't it?

No, it was someone completely out of it on something, I said, someone talking mad drug language, and she broke into my house and stole my boots because someone had stolen hers. Also, I still can't get the birdshit out of the carpet.

Martina Inglis was hooked.

She rubbed her face with her hands, put her hands over her mouth, took them away again.

A girl. I mean, why not? Why would we ever imagine not? There were a few, I bet, there must've been a few. But I bet there weren't many. *Stew pans, locks, hinges, good at decorative.*

She shook her head.

And thrown out for fornicating, well that would definitely have happened. There were smithing apprenticeship rules, fornication's one of the actual forbiddens in the rules, no fornication allowed if you're apprenticed. Also. That burn mark you saw. What shape was it?

Like a bird's open beak, I said. A greater-than sign in maths. Bright red, very inflamed, across the collarbone and chest.

The V-brand, she said. It was for vagrants.
Vagabonds.

She was definitely on the streets, I said.

Ordinance of Labourers 1349, Martina Inglis
said. Then various Vagabonds Acts in the next two
or three hundred years. They burned the letter V
into the skin on the chests or the faces of people
who didn't have a job, or didn't belong to the
parish. The parishes never wanted to have to pay
for anybody extra so they burned all sorts of letters
on to people. The letter V was for anyone homeless,
anyone wandering, like wandering players, I mean
actors, and dancers and performers, entertainers.
They branded what they called Egyptians, that's
where the word Gypsy comes from. Basically
anyone remotely foreign-seeming. They could even
be hanged.

Yeah, but this isn't history, I said. It's now.
It was some poor girl off the street right now.
I literally saw her flinch when she put the Savlon
on the burn.

History too, she said. Happening right now. Do
you think maybe she wasn't saying *you choose*, all
along she was actually saying *new shoes*?

I shrugged.

And the poor laws were specifically there to fix
people's localities, she said. They couldn't rove
around with impunity. They were forced to
work where they'd been registered. The laws first

came in because of the Black Death, because so many people died that the local workforces were really depleted. And then there was the Enclosures Act, taking common land away from common usage, so people couldn't graze animals or find fuel easily any more. Enforced workforce trick. Then a population explosion made vagrants even more plentiful. Even more people to be publicly branded with hot irons, perfect example to keep everybody else in their place.

V for vanquished, I said.

Victimized, she said.

Visitor, I said.

Versus, she said.

Past v present. Us v them, I said.

VIP lane, she said.

Ha, I said. V for that programme called V from the 1980s where power-mad aliens who land in a spaceship in cities all over the world pretend to mean us well then reveal themselves as monsters.

I don't think I saw that, she said. But V for victory, yay!

Voltage, I said.

Velocity, she said.

Virus, I said.

Vaccine, she said.

V for virtual, I said. Nice to talk to you, albeit virtually.

No, don't go, she said. Not yet. V for neck.

For what? I said.

For V-neck. And V for the Korean pop star.

Who? I said.

V, she said. From BTS.

From what? I said.

They're gender neutral, she said. Like one of my kids. They're what we used to call a pop group and they're changing the world one song at a time. So I'm told. They're definitely very dancey.

How do you even know any of this at our great age? I said.

I move with the times, she said.

Talking of which, I said.

I mock-looked at my wrist, where there was no watch.

She nodded. She gave me a serious look across the virtual between.

Thank you, Sand. For your V for visitor imagination, she said.

I told you, I said. It was a real person in my house, really stealing, really wasted, really filthy, really strong-smelling, really hurt, and with a burn on her collarbone that was really weeping.

Martina Inglis nodded again.

I could actually smell that earthburnt smell, she said.

That's a symptom, I said.

And I can see her now working the bellows on a forge, I mean I can see her clearly.

That's another symptom, I said. You should take a test.

You've literally unlocked something, she said. Not just for me. In me. That you'd do that for me. I'll definitely sleep tonight. She said she was a healer, didn't she? You've gifted me a kind of healer. God. I feel weirdly . . . dimensional. How did you do that?

All the best, I said.

I put the cursor over the leave button and pressed it. The screen asked me again. Was I sure I wanted to leave?

I was.

I think I may've been waiting for you all my life, Martina Inglis was saying.

Bye, I said.

I clicked her off.

I switched off the computer.

On my desk next to the screen there was a printout of a painting by William Blake.

In it there's a child standing in a room with a shut door behind it. The shut door takes up the whole picture. The child is thin, off-centre, has clasped hands as if begging or praying, but it's an upright child, not subservient, looking out of the picture right past the heads of anyone looking at the picture as if there's something right behind us, something awful, or awe-ful.

111

The child is saying, without saying anything, the word please.

Across the door behind the child, blocking any getaway, there's a dog much bigger and more substantial than the child and its snout's in the air like it's howling.

Is it dangerous? Is it benign? It's a bit like a massive draught excluder so who knows? All we know about it is its sheer size and the silent howl that's coming from it and passes between it and the child.

There's no getting out of that room. Light is coming through into it from somewhere else but in wedge-shaped shafts like these shafts are forming yet more bars to the door.

A dog starv'd at his Master's Gate / Predicts the ruin of the State.

What I didn't tell Martina Inglis (I uh edited it out) was how I'd also seen that girl go over to the mantelpiece in my bedroom and take the clock my father once gave me off it, the green lacquered clock his mother'd bought in a Woolworths between the wars, and walk in my boots with the clock held away from herself all the way to the window then drop it out of the window so it smashed on the pavement below.

Then the pieces of that clock and I swear I saw this happen had risen by their broken selves into the air and floated up from the street below back to upper window level where they hung outside the house separate in the air but magnetized towards each other as if they might rearrange themselves back into clock-shape – more, as if they were longing to.

Which is what they then did, forming a new clock from the pieces of the old one, the new one patterned with sealed-over cracks like a glazed and aged ceramic.

She'd leaned out the window and reached for the new-old clock, carried it back across the room and put it where it'd originally been on the mantelpiece.

Then she curled asleep on the floor under the bookshelves, her bird a couple of shelves above her on a row of paperbacks with its beak tucked backwards into itself, my father's dog asleep with her head on her paws next to her like the dogs who look after the people on the street who live in the doorways of shops.

It didn't look comfortable for the sleeping girl, on the floor like that, so I imagined her downstairs on the couch under a warm blanket instead, though still attended by the creatures.

Of course, there was no girl there, or bird.

There was only me and my father's dog.

I put a bowl of the dog's favourite brand of dog biscuit, of which I can only afford two days a week's worth, down by her head. I glanced at the cracked clock, saw how late it was. I cleaned my teeth, got into bed, put the light out, head on the pillow, thinking about the word. Brand. Brand new. Brand loyalty. Brand recognition. Brand name. Firebrand.

The letter F was what they burned on to people if they were fighters or fraudsters.

The letter S for slaves. You could claim as your own slave anyone who'd been idle in your parish for more than three days, have them branded with the letter S on the face after which you could legally force them to work for you for no money.

The letter B for blasphemers.

The letter T for thieves.

The letters SL if they were seditious libellers or people who challenged out loud the established order of things or encouraged insurrection against it.

The firebrand in the fire on the forge with the letter V on it glowing white in the heat.

Marked for life.

Forge or forget.

Surface v depth:

and if you said someone was light-timbered it meant they were a weakling, I told my father. That's a good one.

I was telling him, quietly, the hospital air coming in through my mask, about the book of words I'd been reading.

Specifically used by the poor, the rogues and vagabonds, in other words the people shunted to the edge of things in the 1690s, I tell him. A dumb or a dub was a key that could open any lock. A lanspresado was someone who regularly went out drinking with everyone but never brought their wallet. (I imagined him laughing at that one.) And if you like that one, you'll like these. A lord was their word for deformed or crooked people. And a tale-teller was a servant hired to put people to sleep by talking a load of rubbish to them. Or another word for an author.

My father laughing like a storm several fathoms under a sea's surface. My father / not my father in the bed. Visitors were now permitted in the non-virus wards for socially distanced masked and gloved brief visits only. He was in a kind of hiatus between conscious and un, so tired he was still partly elsewhere, his designated nurse, Viola, explained to me. But he'd know I was here, she said. So I was to speak to him. Tell him things, she said.

What else could I tell him?

Curlews actually turn up in one of the earliest English poems we've got, I said into the hope. For instance, in a poem from a thousand years ago, some of the first written-down poetry in English, there's a couple of lines where there's maybe a curlew. The poem's about a person who's miles from land, they've been at sea in a boat for a long long time, and it's a sort of prayer about our aloneness and our surviving. All the seasons pass through it, or the poem's speaker passes in the boat through all the seasons with nothing for company but the sea and the life of the sea. Except, dad, and this is what I love about it, actually that speaker isn't alone at all, *because* I'm reading or hearing the poem, or you are, if it's you reading it. A conversation with someone or something that's silent is still a conversation.

116

Plus, I mean, imagine. Us way out in the future still reading that poem, me sitting here telling you about that poem more than a thousand years after it got written. It fills me with sheer wonder when I think how *not* alone the speaker is every time someone reads that poem. Anyway, down there in the middle of a lonely sea, the person in the boat says that the calls of gannets and the cries of curlews are what have replaced men's laughter for them. In other words, taken the place of the happy noise that happens when people hang out with other people, I said through my mask into the silence round the beeping.

My father, at sea.

Or was it me at sea?

So there's merriment *and* sadness in the sea air both at once, I said. Like merriment and sadness are natural travelling companions. And maybe this person *always* felt stranded and a bit separate, I mean in the company of other people, even when they weren't anywhere near the sea.

I sat with the words I'd said out loud falling away in the hospital air.

Beep.   Beep.

V for visitor.

He was some place I couldn't get into, its windows all dark to me.

Or maybe it was me who was in the dark place and he was in a bright elsewhere.

117

But great conversation we were having, some of the best we'd ever had, ha ha!

He'd laugh about this, wouldn't he? when he came round and I told him all the things he'd had to listen to me holding forth about.

You're beyond me now
to me at school.

You're way beyond me now
to me at university.

It hurt – hurts – the heart.

Now I sat the right distance away at the door of his storeroom.

They call curlews local migrants, I said. Some of them leave the country but others just move themselves seasonally round the UK. Numenius arquata. If their genus name comes from the Greek it's related to how their beaks are curved like a new moon, or an archer's bow. If it comes from the Latin it's maybe also about how curlews are numinous, a sign of divine presence, so that seeing one is sort of like a god's just nodded at you in passing. They're reputed to be the wildest of all birds, completely untameable. And they can live for thirty years. And they're really, really endangered now. The people who care about birds reckon they'll have died out completely in the UK about eight years from now. That's less than a third of the lifespan of a curlew.

A curfew of curlews.

Viola came to signal to me that time was up.

She told me again to call her on her mobile any time night or day if I was worried or wanted an update and that she'd call me immediately if anything, and so on.

I told her again how much I thanked her and how I wished I could hug her.

Soon, she said and her eyes were smiling but very tired.

I went down the stairs and out. I walked over to the car in the car park. But instead of getting in I went to the low fence round the car park in which there were now actual dips in the corrugated metal because so many people had been sitting on it over the last year doing this same thing in the days we weren't allowed in, quite a few of us, at a safe distance from each other, sitting looking up at the building where our people were.

A bus driver.

A dinner lady.

Designs books.

Teacher.

Caught it on the street.

Caught it from my brother.

Caught it God knows how. Shielded till they told shielding people it was safe to go back out.

Came in for a fainting fit and caught it in the hospital.

Marathon runner, health fanatic, never ever ill.

A nurse. So many thank-you cards at home we can't close the bureau drawers.

Garden full of dahlias, wins prizes every year they're that good.

We only ate out the once.

Every day I go over and flush the toilet in his house so the rats won't come up through the system.

We had the best time. We got so drunk and were so happy, and we ran past all the restaurants all the way along the pier to the lighthouse and when we got there we lay on the road holding our stomachs, we were laughing so much, and people kept walking past us and laughing too because we were.

I got better and he hasn't.

My mother. My sister. My father. My brother. My love. My partner. My friend.

I'd nod.

I'd stare up at the building with them and we'd say things like

we're not alone

and

you're not alone.

I knew the grassblades in the broken pavement and the sprig of something (no idea what) forcing its way upwards on the patch of cracked-open tarmac next to the bus shelter.

The weeds growing up the side of that bus shelter were tenacious.

Real v fake:

my father's dog began to bark. She was barking because there was somebody shouting outside the house. I came out of the studio through the house to the front. I looked out the window.

It was one of the Pelf twins.

A HOME WRECKER LIVES HERE, the twin was shouting.

I opened the door. It was the CELINE one, I was pretty sure. Eden.

What are you doing? I said.

I'm telling all the people unfortunate enough to live near you what you really are, she said.

She turned back to the street and she shouted:

THE PERSON WHO LIVES HERE IS A WOKE DELUDED DEGENERATE USING

THE PANDEMIC AS AN EXCUSE FOR
DEBAUCHERY.

A small group of my neighbours had gathered
outside their houses on the other side of the street.
Steve was there, and Carlo, and Marie and
Jaharanah, and Madison and Ashley. I waved to
them. They waved back.

You okay, Sand? Jaharanah called over.

So far, I said.

Then I started shouting too.

THIS PERSON SHOUTING OUTSIDE MY
HOUSE IS A PITTIKINS.

What did you just call me? Eden Pelf said.

SHE'S A CULVER, I shouted. A HEART'S
ROOT. A CRYSTAL BUTTON.

Stop calling me those names! she said.

She started to cry.

What does pittikin mean? she asked. How dare
you say you pity me.

Look. Do you want a cup of tea? I said. Stay
here. I'll bring you one.

I WANT YOU TO DIE, she shouted in tears.

She was sobbing now.

What've you done with my mother? she said
through the sobs.

Is your mother still missing? I said.

No, Eden said. She's home. But it's like. It's like
even though she's there she's no one we know any
more.

122

Before I could step away from her she'd collapsed against me in tears and was holding on to me.

Oh Christ, I said. Oh no.

I held my arms out away from her.

I really need to sit down, she said. I think I'm going to faint.

I opened the front windows wide and sat her down in the front room. I went to wash my hands. When I came back and stood in the doorway she was looking round at the shelves.

So many books, she said.

A lot less than there were, I said. I'm slowly whittling them down.

Why? she said.

I'm getting older, I said.

That's a weird thing to say, she said.

Thanks, I said.

Do you double-you eff aitch? she said. I do.

I don't know. Do I? I said.

It means work from home, she said.

Ah. Yes, I said. I've a workshop in the studio in the garden.

What, that old shed? she said.

That old shed, I said.

What do you do? she said.

I'm a painter, I said.

And decorator?

No, I said. The other kind.

Are you on furlough from that job? she said.

No, I said. I'm on emergency rations.

I was, at first, she said. But then last year we got a big new contract so admin went crazy and we had to organize things we'd no idea how to do and we kept getting it wrong.

Right. How do you take your tea? I said.

I don't want tea, she said. I don't want anything. Everything tastes horrible.

Ah, I said. Uh oh.

Like something's rotten, she said. I've got this burning feeling and this smell at the back of my nose that makes everything the same. I've had it for two months. It makes me not want to eat anything ever again.

Were you ill for long? I said.

I wasn't ill at all, she said. I don't get ill. One day for some reason I just stopped being able to taste like I used to be able to. And now I can't even taste things that have a lot of taste in them like spicy things. Never mind just enjoy a piece of bread any more.

It'll heal, I said. Apparently it does, in time, the taste and smell thing.

But what if it doesn't? she said.

You'll maybe have to live with that possibility for a while, I said.

Her face went all despair.

I hate it, she said. I want how I taste things to go back to how it was before. I want everything to go back to how it was before.

I sat down on the arm of the furthest-away chair at the other side of the room.

You're going to make some joke about me being tasteless now, like Lea does, she said.

I think we're all under quite a lot of pressure, I said. I think there's a lot of raw feeling in the air, and not just because there's been so much illness. I think there's a great deal of despair around, and even more anger than there was before.

Eff wy eye I'm not angry, she said drying her tears on a sleeve.

She said it angrily.

I think we've been taking in anger like sponges for half a decade now, I said. This isn't the first time that someone's stood outside my house shouting.

Wreck their fam dynamic too, did you? she said.

I was sitting in that chair you're in now, one day a couple of years BC, before covid, I was just sitting there reading a book, I said. And a woman and a man I didn't know and have never seen again started yelling outside. I realized after a minute they were yelling at my front room window. At me. So I opened the window. I asked them what the matter was. The woman told me my front room had made her feel really angry. Then the man said I was lazy. I had no idea what they were talking about. Then I realized they were angry at my books.

They were shouting at your books? Eden Pelf said.

Funny, I said. When I was a kid I used to think lining a room with books was one of the most exciting things anyone could do to a room.

What did you say to them? she said.

I told them I thought books were important, I said.

Why? Eden said.

Uh, I said. Well. Because I think they are. And they told me I was scum, a waste of space, and I told them space was never wasted, and the man told me to shut my face and the woman told me to stop aggressing him by answering back, then they went away. And I went back to my book.

No, I meant why *are* books important? she said.

Apart from that they're a pleasure? I said. Because, uh, because they're one of the ways we can imagine ourselves otherwise.

Why would we ever want to do that? Eden said.

Why wouldn't we? I said.

Is that what you've done to our mother? she said.

Pff, I said.

Eden was glancing round the room now as if for clues, up at the ceiling, at the doors leading through to the back, as if to deduce whether I had several people's mothers locked in the house somewhere. But then –

Oh! she said.

She took a book off the shelf next to her.

The Cottingley Fairies! she said. How do you know about the Cottingley Fairies?

Hundred-year-old fake news, I said.

I can't believe it, she said.

She sat and flicked through it.

I loved these, she said. I did a project about them, a dissertation. It was all tied up with the aftermath of a war. All the people dead, and people wanting to believe that fairies were real. I haven't thought about them for years.

She put the book on her knee.

What's amazing, she said, is that nobody could prove they were faked for so long including the guy who wrote Sherlock Holmes, I mean the books not the TV series, and he said that looking at these pictures got the British people out of a muddy rut. Well. He didn't *want* them to be faked. He believed in ghosts and all that rubbish.

She opened the book again.

I love how the fairies in the pictures had really modern, I mean for the time, hairstyles, look –

She bent it wide open and held it up towards me.

– and how it looks in this one like the fairy the girl's looking at, I can't remember which girl she is, Emily or the other one, is offering her a flower and it looks so real, the whole thing, how clever they were. I mean they were just little kids with nothing else to do one summer. And they fooled the whole world. Imagine you having a book. About them. When I was small, I mean Amelie's age, I really believed in them, not just these ones in the photos, I believed in them generally. When I think of how much I believed in them. I used to think that when leaves rustled in bushes in the breeze, that that's what it would sound like when they talked to each other. But obviously I also knew it wasn't true at the same time. I really enjoyed doing that dissertation about them, I did it in art, at schoo –

She had cracked its spine too far and the book split in two in her hands.

Oh no. Oh. I'm really sorry.

No matter, I said. Really don't worry, don't worry at all.

I'm so embarrassed. I've ruined it. I'll get you another one, she said.

No need, I said. In fact, you can have it, if you like. Both of it. I don't need to read it again.

She stared at me.

What, to keep?

Yes, I said.

I couldn't possibly, she said.

Up to you, I said. If you'd like it. Otherwise it'll go in the recycling.

She started to cry again.

I'm sorry, she said. It's the thought of fairies, even if they're not real, in the recycling. And those girls from a hundred years ago. Real girls once. In the recycling.

She put her hand in her CELINE bag and took her phone out at the same time as a handful of tissues.

Oh. Oh no. Oh, what? That's really weird, she said.

She looked at her phone, swiped at it.

It's dead, she said.

She pressed it. Nothing. She pressed it again.

It's weird. It's just completely dead, she said. Look. What's wrong with it?

Panic went all through her.

Flat battery, I said.

I charged it this morning, she said. This shouldn't be happening, it just shouldn't be happening, it can't happen, it's wrong, it's really wrong.

She shook it. She pressed it again.

Oh God, she said. Oh no.

Probably just rebooting, I said.

It won't, she said. I can't get it to.

She pressed something. She shook it. She pressed it again.

Let me try, I said.

I came across the room, stretched my own hand as far away from myself as I could. I took the phone, held the on button down and counted to fifteen. The phone lit up.

No way! she said. How did you get it to do that? Oh thank God.

Just keep this button here pressed down for longer if it happens again, I said.

She put the broken book in her bag and stood up.

Gee tee gee, she said. That's got to go.

Whatever you say, I said.

Gee tee ar, she said. That's got to run.

At the front door she turned.

Thanks. For sorting my phone, she said.

Nothing to do with me, I said. It was the fairies.

She looked startled. Then she gave me a huge grin.

I watched her go down to the bottom of the street and get into a car and shut the door, I watched her drive off. Then I shut my own door, disinfected my hands and went to have a bath.

Tragedy v farce:

I was sitting over by the window taking a break from a Dylan Thomas poem I was working on.

I'd been layer-painting this poem since the start of the pandemic, in whites then greens then golds then more whites then reds and now finally greens. By coincidence I'd layered the words *curlews* and *curlew* into it months ago, not words I'd ever even thought about before these years or this poem.

In it Dylan Thomas conjures all the desire and longing there's ever been in all the people who've ever lived and died and turned to dust and in us still living who'll die in our turn and in all the people after us who'll ever live and die. Then he imagines that longing as a fire in the dark that'll never stop burning and he tosses curlew imagery into the sky all through the poem.

I'd been working from first word towards last. I was on the second last word, *fires*. After it there'd only be the word *still* still to do. These last words were and would be green and I was thinking about the notion of green fire, what happened when those two words came together, when the word *scarlet* lit up the spine of a book on the bookshelf next to my head.

What book was that?

The Scarlet Letter.

I took it off the shelf.

It was a paperback as old as me and still pristine. Nobody'd yet read this book, including me. I'd bought it in a Saturday market from a second hand bookstall more than forty years ago and it had been on my shelves in all the places I'd lived since, unopened.

I opened it.

10p in pencil on the inside cover. Underneath that, someone had written in red biro the words

To you, in admiration, Nathaniel Hawthorne.

A joke, clearly.

Anyway it had ended up very unread and on a second hand stall so whoever gave whoever this book, they didn't get or didn't like or didn't want the joke.

I knew a little about the story; it's a classic novel. Maybe that's why I'd never read it. Maybe I thought I knew it all already.

What if, next time, I painted a novel rather than a poem?

Maybe by the time I'd finished painting something as long as this novel we'd all be well into whatever the next stage of this time in our lives would shape up to be, through the tragedy, past the farce.

First page:

A throng of bearded men, in sad-coloured garments and grey steeple-crowned hats, inter-mixed with women, some wearing hoods, and others bareheaded, was assembled in front of a wooden edifice, the door of which was heavily timbered with oak, and studded with iron spikes.

Sad-colour. Church clothes. Men and women, some bare-headed, so, something scandalous happening. Heavy door. Spikes.

I glanced down the page.

Utopia. Cemetery. Prison.

I turned the page.

Rose-bush. History.

Pluck one of its flowers and present it to the reader.

Oh, that's good.

Would I go first word to last or last word to first?

Going start to finish in transferring a text into oils has a weighty heft, is physically conclusive, can be satisfying. It can also feel too fixed and closed and completed. Going finish to start can feel precipitous, unsafe. But the finished work can be liberated by the knowledge that the finished surface you meet with your eyes is a beginning, not an end. Partly, though, in the process, it's like you're reversing along a motorway at a crazy speed while all the other cars are going fast forwards round you.

Whichever way, it's all about the building up of the layers.

Something dimensional happens, a bit like the thing that happens between words themselves, their physical realization and the physical objects we call books.

I checked its last page:

our now concluded legend; so sombre is it, and relieved only by one ever-glowing point of light gloomier than the shadow: – 'ON A FIELD, SABLE, THE LETTER A, GULES.'

Gules.

Gules is a red colour to do with heraldry. It's a word Shakespeare uses for blood, or the colour of blood. He uses it in Hamlet and that word sable with it too, when he's describing a warrior first hidden in the dark inside of the Trojan horse, then outside covered in the blood of the families he murders. The warrior is called Pyrrhus. As in pyrrhic victory.

If I started with the end of the book, then, I'd surface with rose colour overlaid with *sad-coloured* (I'd have to decide what sad-coloured means since

no colour is inherently sad). Whereas if I started
at the start we'd surface in a bright heraldic
blood red.

I was just about to look up on my phone to see if
I was imagining that the name Pyrrhus also
happens to mean red, particularly the burning red
colour of a fire, when

knock knock.

Front door.

Dog, barking.

A Pelf twin was on the welcome mat.

This face was full of resolve. It was Lea. There
was a quite large holdall at their feet.

Going somewhere nice? I said.

I didn't know where else to go, Lea said.

Lockdown. It's tough, I said. I'm so sorry. But
there are still ways to get out of the country. Or a,
what's it called. Staycation.

No, I mean I'm homeless. He's thrown me out.

Who has? I said.

Lea raised their eyebrows at me.

Apparently I'm not a proper girl, they said. And
I'll never be the son and heir he wanted. And
various other clichés. Well. He's right.

I thought he'd already thrown you out, I said.

I was living in the workroom above the garage.
Banished. To make me see sense. But because it
didn't make me see sense he wants me banished
from the garage now too. I sully his Audi.

Oh dear, I said. Where's your mother in all this? What does she think?

Isn't she here with you? Lea said.

No, I said.

Oh, Lea said.

Uncomfortable pause.

Lea Pelf stood saying nothing.

Then:

my sister says you were really nice to her when she came round.

Yes, she did come round, I said.

Lea shifted from foot to foot.

Don't know where else to go.

You've got friends, I said.

Nobody uncomplicated enough, Lea said.

Work colleagues, I said. You must have money. With your high-flying eye tee eye gee job.

I don't have colleagues as such. I work from home. Well, I did. Then I worked from garage. I'm a drone, really, it's not high-flying. I'm only a junior level human eye.

What's that mean? I said.

I scan stuff for several companies to check for things that digiscans might have missed or misread, to make sure nobody can sue them. Human eye pays peanuts at junior level.

So you must be legally trained, I said.

No. They just send us a download of the list of things to watch out for. If we see anything on the

list in any of the content we forward it to the
lawyers and their own human eyes. I'm supposed to
be doing it right now. I've got to meet the daily.

Daily what?

Ratio.

Lea wrapped their arms round themself, cold.

Where's your coat? I said.

At home. In the garage, Lea said. I just. Got on a
train and came here.

There must be warm places you can go and sit and
work, I said. What about the library? Oh, oh no.

I'd forgotten the library was luxury flats now.

I've actually got a friend who lives in the old
reading room, Lea said. Amazing architecture.
Vaulted ceiling.

There you go. You could go there, I said.

Well, not a friend. A boss really. I don't really
know him. God, if they thought at work that I'd
nowhere to work. They'll be checking my ratios
right now. The machines watch us, I was going to
say like hawks but it's worse, they watch us like
machines. They report back every twenty minutes
about what and how much, and we get flagged and
rated daily.

Cafes, I said. They're nice and warm. Those
burners outside. Hotel lounges, free wifi, bit of
glamour. Are hotel lounges letting people in
again now?

You seem so cool, like a goddess, Lea said.

I what? I said.

You seem like you really get it, Lea said.

Lea was bright red in the face.

Uh, I said. You can't stay here. You can't even come *in* here.

It was kind of you to let Eden in, Lea said.

I was forced to, I said. By her emotional state.

Sandy, you're so great. You stood up to my father about my emotional state. You told him loud and clear down the phone. You weren't intimidated. You were magnificent. You said it and he had to listen. You're a catalyst. You're an avatar. You've transformed our mother into a live person. She was like dead till now. You're what our family's needed all this time. You're amazing.

Please, I said. Lea. Stop it.

I think you're the reason he threw me out, Lea said.

Don't try manipulative narrative with me, I said, I'm wise to it.

You *are* wise, Lea said. I don't think I've ever met anybody as wise as you before.

You've spent less than twenty minutes in my company, I said.

It doesn't take more than a moment to know, Lea said.

That's madness, I said.

But Lea was looking at their phone. Colour drained from their face.

Oh God, they said.

What? I said.

It's work. I told you. I've been marked down twice now for absent ratio. Oh God.

Lea sat down on my doorstep and unzipped the holdall, took out a laptop.

Just let me sign in and ghost out some ratio for a minute, they said.

It started to rain. Lea got a white shirt out of their bag and draped it over their head and over the laptop.

The rain got really really heavy. Tap tap tap. The shirt was transparent with rain now. I could see Lea clearly under it.

Look, I said. You can do this in my hall. Here. Sit there. Don't come near me. Over there. On the stairs. No, leave the door open.

Thanks, they said. Unbelievable kindness. I know the pressure you're under, Sand. You're the real thing. Have you got a hairdryer?

No. Well, yes, I said, but you can't have it.

Lea, dripping rain on to the old parquet, hung the wet shirt over the banister, sat down on the third step up and keyboarded. I put on a mask. I sat right back in the hall by the kitchen door. The cold spring air came through the house and kept me wary.

Twenty minutes passed.

I checked my phone.

Nothing hospital-based.

No Viola.

Rain fell into the house and darkened the floor by the door.

I checked it again.

Nothing hospital-based.

No Viola.

You know, Lea said as they tippy tapped. You should really have a website.

I don't want a website, I said.

There's stuff about you online, about your pictures, the art thing. You paint words on top of each other. That's cool. The pictures are kind of amazing. They look like they're three dimensional. Like a club sandwich.

See? There's more than enough about me online already, I said.

But you're not utilizing it, Lea said. I can put you in touch with a couple of influencers. It'll cost you. Money well spent.

Just as a matter of interest, Lea, I said. What *can* you find out about people online if, like you, you know where to look?

God, yeah. Anything, Lea said. Everything.

Like what? I said.

What do you need? Lea said. Work address? Home address? Webmail? Medical details? Passport stuff. Number of children. Educational level. Children's educational level. Gross annual income in any currency. Credit card purchases. What categories you're in re financials and lifestyle. Hobbies. Interests. Voting intentions. Religious and political alliances. What you watch. What you browse. What you eat. How much alcohol you drink at home. Syntactical patterning. Sexual proclivities.

Can it really tell you about syntactical patterning? I said.

Devices, Lea said. They're key. To everything. On everyone. Alive or dead.

They went back to tippy tapping.

Knock knock at the open front door.

The dog started to bark again.

It was the other Pelf twin on the doorstep under an umbrella.

Is the dog shut in the kitchen? she said.

Yes, I said.

Why are you wearing that mask? she said.

Because there's a pandemic, I said.

There's more to life than just this boring pandemic. Masks really upset me. Seeing people wear them has a negative effect on my mental health. Aren't you going to take it off? Now that you've seen it's just me?

No, I said. What can I do for you, Eden?

I came because I thought you might like to see this, she said.

She held out what looked like a school jotter.

Rain hit its blue cover and left large splotches next to her name.

I had to come because I was feeling really really bad, she said. That I got that girl's name wrong the other day. I said it was Emily. It wasn't Emily, it was Elsie. It really upset me to get it so wrong, I've actually had trouble sleeping. So I started looking through all my things from when I was younger. Oh, hi Lea.

Hi, Lea said without looking up.

I went through everything, I thought maybe it'd been thrown out when they converted the loft, I was dreading finding out that it wasn't there, she said. But it was! It was back behind the divide in the unconverted rafters, it was at the bottom of a black plastic bag behind the paint tins. How do the things that mattered more than anything else, the things that meant so much to us at the time, end up in the plastic bag tucked at the back of the paint tins in the unconverted bit of the loft? Eye dee kay. That means I don't know.

She opened the jotter.

Large round schoolchild handwriting. Circles over the i's. Drawings. Cuttings printed off the internet and sellotaped in. Faded printouts of photos.

She got to the middle pages and folded out two much larger pages decorated to look like wings, as if the project book itself was a winged thing. She smiled an open-mouthed smile at me.

Lea stood up and stretched.

I just want to nip back to the garage and collect something, they said. I won't be long.

You can't come back here, I said.

Ede, have you got the car? Lea said.

Eden handed Lea a car key and pointed to where the car was parked down the street. I looked at the name of the school on the jotter. It was a school in a city nearly two hundred miles away.

Brr, Eden said as she watched Lea run. Cold today.

She stepped into the house. I backed further down the hall.

Please don't come into the house, I said.

But Lea was in the house, she said. Were you telling them a story? Because if you were then I want one too. It's *okay*, I'm *well*. I'm *completely fine*. We can go in your book lounge and sit miles away from each other like last time.

How about you maybe leave your project book with me and I'll read it and we can talk about it when I give it back to you the next time I see you, I said.

You could read it right now, she said.

I'm busy right now, I said.

Lea's taken the car, she said. I'll have to wait for them to come back.

You can't wait here, I said.

Where else would I go? she said.

There are cafes, I said.

It's *way* too cold and wet to sit outside a cafe, she said. I'll *die*.

If Lea's gone home maybe you should too, I said.

They'll be back. They've left their stuff, she said.

The wet shirt, the open holdall spilling out clothes and computer gear, were still at the bottom of the stairs. Eden meanwhile was already wandering about flicking her wet hair behind her shoulders in the front room.

Oh for fuck sake, I said.

I crossed behind her and opened the window then came and sat in the stiff breeze as far away from her as possible.

The Scarlet Letter, she was saying as she sat down. That sounds good.

She'd picked it up off the arm of the sofa.

What's it about? she said.

I've never read it, I said. But I know it's about a woman who has to wear a, a letter, on her chest, I think because she's had a child with someone she's not married to.

God. I hope it wasn't a long letter, that'd be really annoying hanging off your clothes all the time, Eden said.

No, not a letter *from* someone. A letter of the alphabet. The letter A. Bright red. A for adulteress, I said.

Romantic, Eden said. Like a laundress, or an air

144

hostess, or a seamstress. Adulteress. Someone from the past who works with adults.

No, well, I said, adulteress is –

Oh em gee! Eden said. It's signed! By its author!

Uh, I said. Please don't bend the page back like that.

Is it worth a lot? Eden said. I know, right? Like this is, to me.

She put The Scarlet Letter down and picked up her jotter again. She opened it. Then she started reading out loud:

once there were two girls called Frannie and Elsie. They had different surnames and this is because they were cousins. They were bored one boring summer and one of them it isn't clear which one from the extensive reading I did for this project but I suspect it was the older taller one because the drawings are very good and quite mature so probably the older one did the drawings of fairies and she stuck hat pins through them so it looked like they were really standing up on a tree log in the grass and taking a sun bath then the girls from Cottingley took photographs of them as if they were really there and exist and they became known as the Cottingley Fairies when their Fame spread. Kodak was fooled Kodak was a major photographery company and knew about photographs and even they could not tell they were faked. Either the photographs or the fairies. A man

called Arthur Doyle was fooled he famously wrote
about the British hero Sherlock Holmes and he
wanted fairies and mysterious things to be real
because his stories were full of them so more
people would believe his stories were true thus he
did a lot of publicity for the fairies which were
beautiful and lifelike with beautiful wings even
though they were fake he said that the British
People wanted to think about the wings of fairies
and not be stuck any more in a muddy rut of war.
This is because it was in a time when there was a
first world war happening in 1920 and people were
upset that their world views were changing and
farmers were upset that their fields were being
churned into mud and sometimes the farmers that
are farming those fields even today in the faraway
country of the ee you which we are now leaving
where those wars were fought still find pieces of
dead bones when they are planting crops for

Knock knock.

Dog, barking.

Eden looking terrified.

Okay! I call through to the dog. Enough!

The dog stopped barking.

Oh, Eden said.

She was next to the window and could see who was at the door. She gave me a long sorrowful look.

I went to the front door. Martina Inglis's eyes above the mask. The lines round them were new but they met my own eyes with the same old challenge.

Want to come out somewhere with me in my fast car?

Where? I said.

It's a secret, she said.

She had a pair of ice skates hanging by their laces tied together round her neck.

Is it ice skating? I said.

Your local icerink, she said, is not yet accepting members of the public but they recognized my name, I used to be a quite well known medal winner and the manager's the same age as us so I rang him up, my name rang a bell for him and he did me the favour. An icerink to ourselves. I can't wait to show you my moves. God, Sand, it's amazing to see you in person. Isn't it amazing? I feel ecstatic, I feel wild and free, I feel young again. This is the furthest from home I've been for a year. So this is where you live. Where did she sleep? Which lampshade did the bird knock into with its wings? I'm looking forward to seeing the actual lampshade.

Mum, Eden said. What are you doing here?

Oh, Martina Inglis said. Eden.

Yeah, Eden said. Me.

What are you doing here? Martina Inglis said taking off her mask and putting it in her coat pocket.

I'm reading to her from my Cottingley Fairies project, Eden said. At least *she's* interested in my life. You haven't answered me. Why are *you* here?

I'm here to take my old university friend skating, Martina Inglis said.

I can't skate, I said. Why don't you take your daughter?

Martina Inglis ignored me.

Who's looking after Amelie? she said to Eden.

Dad is, Eden said. Plain to see you're not. Though it's your afternoon to.

I left them arguing between the front door and the hall. I slipped into the front room, picked up The Scarlet Letter and slipped it back into its place on the shelf. Then I went to the kitchen, washed my hands. I phoned Viola's mobile and left a message saying I'd get tested before I'd come in again and asked her to give my father my love.

I got the dog and the lead.

Don't wait for me to come back, I said. Please just both leave as soon as you can. Close the front window and make sure the door's locked behind you, will you?

The dog and I got into my car, dog in the passenger seat. They were still arguing at the door when we drove off.

My father's dog's name, by the way, was Shep.

I presume Shep's short for Shepherd and something to do with sheepdogs.

My father has always called all his dogs Shep. This Shep was his fifth. He names them after an old country and western song about dogs and their fidelity. In the song the dog saves his owner from drowning when he's a boy. *To the rescue he came.* Then the day comes when the local dog-doctor tells the owner he can't do no more for him, Jim, and Jim's supposed to shoot Shep to put him out of his misery. He picks up his gun and aims it at Shep's faithful head. But he just can't do it. He wants to run. He wishes they'd shoot him instead. Anyway, Shep does die in the end though it's not clear how, and the song assures us that if dogs have a heaven then Shep's at home there and it's a wonderful afterlife.

I sang what I could remember of it as we drove.

You're an old story in a new form, I said to my father's dog when I got to the end of the song.

She and I exchanged a look.

Shep, I said. I know hallucination's one of the symptoms with this virus. I'm ill, aren't I? I'm hallucinating Pelfs. I'm inventing the opposite of isolation precisely so that I won't mind isolation. Yes?

Shep looked back at me with an unhurried unworried eye.

Like I'm hallucinating a government, I said, running this country so *successfully*, with such calculated ineptness that we've one of the top death tolls per capita in the world. Of course it can't be real. Why didn't I think of that? No wonder it feels so surreal. I'm just – making it up.

Shep eyed the dashboard indifferently.

Or was everything pre-covid the hallucination, and this is the revelation of real realities? I said.

Shep yawned.

I caught the yawn and yawned too.

When we got near my father's house she began to bark and jump about in her seat. When we got to the house she was overjoyed, leapt round and round in circles the size of her own body on the seat, circles that shook the car. When I let her out she jumped the front gate, arthritic hips and all.

She stood with her head pressed against the front door till I opened it. She went through the house checking all the rooms looking for him. She checked both gardens. She came back in and settled under the kitchen table, waited there with her eyes all resignation and duty as if that's what the story of life was, a patient matter of waiting and then the person you're waiting for comes home.

With any luck, I said. Eh?

I patted her head and scruffed her neck.

I'm sorry I've been so unfriendly, I said. My problem, not yours. I'll do better from now on.

I gave her half the tin of beans I heated up for myself. I'm not sure that was completely wise, but no grief came of it, at least none that I knew about, and it felt a companionable thing to do. Then she and I sat in the room that smelt most like my father and watched some TV together.

What we watched was politicians arguing with each other while people drowned in the narrow patch of sea between here and the rest of Europe. The politicians were making themselves huge, as bloated as barrage balloons, possibly because they wanted to suggest the people in the water were comparatively negligible, too small even to be real people, so that the argument would shift from being about people's lives and deaths and become instead about which of the barrage balloon politicians would win an argument.

I was shouting at the screen so loud that my father's dog started to howl. So I switched it off.

Is there such a thing, Shep, as evil? I asked her.

Oh yes, Shep said.

What does it look like? I said.

Well, it's very everyday, really, Shep said. And you're all capable of it. You humans. As well as good.

Are creatures other than humans capable of these things too? I said.

That's an interesting question, Shep said with one paw dandling over the other off the couch in a very poised but casual way. The difference is the point at which time and language meet. Networks of abstract and real meaning, plus how you humans

can and do hold concepts and notions about real
pasts and imagined futures in your use of verbal
language, all this allowing you to weigh sequence
and consequence, experience and different
possibilities, all of which gives you an inbuilt
philosophical impetus, experiential grounding and,
yes, means that for you there's a question of
forethought, imagination and choice when it comes
to how you act. Let's start with evil. But how to
define evil? Hmm. Take cruelty, let's call one aspect
of it the conscious choice or decision to cause pain
to another living being, the forethought at the core
of this definition. A decision made, abstractly and /
or physically, to be cruel, by a being who has a
choice to be or not to be it. Now, we're different.
It's not that we don't have an understanding of
experience. We do, of course, and we learn. And
it's not that we don't have our own conception of
what's right and wrong, as well as the cultural
inheritance of what you tell us *you* think is right
and wrong, at least the more tamed of us who end
up having to listen to you about such things. It's
more that –

I woke up.

Shep's sleeping head was on my knee.

My phone was buzzing next to Shep's head.

Not the hospital or Viola. Unknown number.

Yes? I said.

Hi, the real or imagined Lea said. It's Lea. Will

you be back soon? Only, Eden wants to put Amelie to bed and she's not sure where'd be best.

Is Amelie at my house now too? I said. When are you leaving?

Our father brought her over, Lea said. Eden was freaking out about being separated from her all day.

So why didn't she just go home? I said. Is your father there now too?

He's here, Lea said, but I'm not letting him into the house. He's outside in his car. He can sleep out there. See how he likes it. There's no way he's getting in here.

Why? I said.

This isn't his space, Lea said. In your absence I'm deciding who's in and who's out. Here he's out. Where are you, by the way?

I'm at eh my friend Shep's house, I said. It's quite cold tonight. It'll be cold out there, I mean for your father, in the car.

If he's cold he can easily drive home, Lea said.

He could drive you all home, I said.

Anyway the car's got an excellent heating system. It's a big car. I can hear him, he's still arguing like a madman out there, Lea said.

With whom? I said.

Get you, grammar queen. I love that about you. Nobody says that stuff any more. Yeah, him and my mother are having their usual rant. I think the claustrophobia makes it more exciting. There's nowhere to go in your house. Oh yeah and we had trouble getting your oven to work. Does it work? And have you got a toaster for the morning? We ate without you, I hope you don't mind. We had a takeaway. He ate his in the car. We phoned that curry place you've got the flyer for on the cupboard door in your galley kitchen.

It's a kitchen kitchen, I said.

We all thought it was a quite good curry, except Eden, she couldn't taste it, and I don't know what *he* thought. But I think it's done us all good to get away. Get out of the same house. It's ages since we've all been together in a place we don't know already. Change of scene.

Actually I need you all to get out of my house, I said.

When are you coming back? I know our mother wants to talk to you. She was wandering round the house picking things up and putting them down like it's a sacred site or something. And Eden wants to talk to you about how she was bullied by some really horrible girls when she was at school.

Oh dear. Poor Eden, I said.

And where's the key to the shed? they said. So I can take some photos of your pictures and your working process for the website?

Listen, I said. Your mother and father and sister and you, you too, all of you. None of you will find any answers in my house, or in me. I'm not the

154

story here. You're not the story. Do you hear me? We're not the story. In any case, a story is never an answer. A story is always a question.

Yeah but you can't say that. You don't know, Lea said.

I know some things. I'm older than you, I said.

Can I ask you politely not to be ageist? Lea said.

These are fragile times, I said. Go out to the car. Make up with your father. Invite him and your mother in. Open one of the bottles of wine in my uh galley. Open them all, if you like, and toast each other, wish each other well. If you don't, one day you'll wish you had. And then, *all of you. Go home*. Please.

Silence.

Then Lea said,

with respect, Sandy, it's nice of you and all, and I know you believe you're some kind of storytelling symbolic avatar in our family or whatever. But you don't have the right to tell the story of me in that patronizing way, however well-meaning you think you are. Or to second guess what I think about my journey or my story or how I should narrate to other people my own quite massive and yes really pretty wild narrative of what it's been like to be me, and I think when I say this I'm speaking for my whole family, and how they'd feel themselves about each of their own truths, whether you designate their truths lesser stories or not. Except my father.

His is definitely not a story I countenance because he hasn't countenanced mine.

I think I'm an avatar, do I? I said.

Symbolic, Lea said.

Right, I said. I'll tell you what this symbolic avatar thinks.

Yeah, thing is you've been telling us nothing *but* what you think since we met, to be honest, and it's getting a bit wearing, Lea said. And I think, if you'll accept some respectful advice, your problem here might be connected to the fact that you don't know or haven't yet admitted who or what you are.

Any *problem here*, I said, might stem from the fact that I've been dropped feet first against my will and at a really dangerous time into some English seaside resort theatrical farce where I've no choice but to –

Yeah but you can't call one of the most landlocked places in England a seaside resort, Lea said. I'd never be seen dead ordering fish in a restaurant here. If restaurants were open again and serving fish.

Message from me, I said. To all of you. Get the fuck out of my house. Right now.

Look, I'm really sorry if I've offended you, Sandy, Lea said. It's late now, and Amelie's just got off to sleep, to be honest it's been hell for Ede, Amelie's been grouching all day, she always is when she's left with our father, and we live a long drive away and anyway as you well know because we've already discussed it I've got nowhere else to live right now. Moreover the only reason we're all still here is because we've been waiting all night for you to come back. And now you say you're *not* coming back. I mean, you could've told us earlier. It's quite impolite of you that you didn't.

Christ almighty, I said. Me. Impolite. You're all in my house against my –

No, I told you, my parents are outside in my father's car, Lea said.

– and your being in there means I *can't* be, because I can't be near anyone in case I contract something that then might hurt my very unwell father –

Ah, okay. That explains your father fixation, Lea said.

My *what*? I said.

Hi, Lea said. It's me.

Yeah, I know who you are, I said, and I know who I am too, and that accusation of a father fixation is sheer transference. If you'd any idea who I am other than your own fictions about me you'd know that actually I have a mother fixation. But that's not a part of this story.

No. It's *me*, it's *Eden*, the real / imagined Eden said. Where *are* you? I've got so much to tell you. Amelie's here. She's longing to meet you. She wants you to tell her a story. She's very keen to get into your shed and play with the paints.

Oh Christ, I said. That's all I need.

Maybe when you get back you'll show us where the key is. And Rory's on his way.

Who's Rory? I said.

My partner. Amelie's father. I know he'd love to meet you too, he's been abroad on business for my dad, he landed half an hour ago, he's on the Heathrow Express.

He'll have to quarantine, I said. Don't let him into my house.

Oh, he'll be fine, en bee dee, Sandy. That means no big deal. We never get ill in our family. And we all know each other so no precautions necessary. My father wants to talk to you too. Not about your and my mother's relationship or anything, don't worry, it's a work thing, he reckons he's had one of his visions and that this is a neighbourhood ripe for pelfing, and he's always right about these things, he's got a sixth sense. He wants to ask you about it.

Ripe for pelfing, I said.

I don't know if you know, Eden said. Apart from the new PPE manufacture initiative and the daily running of Insectex he's also a really well known property developer.

I don't actually own the house that your whole family's just taken over, I said. I only rent it.

Uh huh, we know, Eden said, we've already been in touch with the guy who owns most of your street. But my father thinks you might be able to talk generally, be a horse's mouth he says though God knows what that's supposed to mean, and tell him things about what it's like, you know, the ups and downs of living in the neighbourhood.

The neighbourhood.

Steve, who has a full-sized skeleton from his days as a medic and kept it in the passenger seat of his van till people walking past complained their children were scared of it and that it gave them virus nightmares. So Steve moved it into his house instead and now it gazes out of the front window sporting seasonal accoutrements, a boater and a bow tie for summer, a Santa hat and tinsel at Christmas. Children now regularly congregate outside Steve's house laughing and pointing and taking selfies with it behind them.

Carlo, the bus driver and part-time lecturer in creative writing for people who take the courses he runs for no money in the summer months at the botanical gardens.

Marie and Jaharanah, who work in the care system and are looking older than I've ever seen them, grimmer and grimmer, more and more worn down, the lights in their house are on day and night and even though they've been working endless shifts they still deliver food every day in their beaten-up Mini to people who can't leave the house and have been delivering the occasional bag of groceries to me too since my father, and I don't even know how they know.

Madison and Ashley, the youngest of our neighbours. All I know about them is that they're a couple and they always wave and say a friendly hi though we haven't met properly yet.

Eden, meanwhile, had clearly been talking about something traumatic that happened to her when she was at school.

I think it was envy. They were all envious of me, she was saying.

Character forming, I said.

I know, right? she said. I knew *you'd* understand.

When are you all leaving? I said. And how do you know I rent my house? That's private information.

Well duh. It's online, Eden said.

Which reminds me, hi, it's Lea again, Lea said taking back control of the phone. That website you commissioned me to do.

I didn't commission you to do anything, I said.

Yeah you did. I brought my other computer back this afternoon, I can do it easily now, Lea said. If you can tell me how to open the shed. I've already taken some images of the outside of it, and some of your living spaces I thought'd be relevant, some alcoves, trinkets on your bedside table, things in the bathroom etc. But if you can gather photos or screengrabs of your past works so we can include them all in a timeline, and can you do a career timeline separately with CV stuff on it, that'd be good, also contacts etc, and you'll need to write a brief biog or I can do it for you from what's on the net already.

I don't want a website, I said. I don't give you or any of your family permission to go into my studio, I don't give you permission to take any images of anything to do with my life or work, and I don't give you permission to construct a website for me.

Yeah but you really can't be an artist without a website, Lea said. What are you laughing at?

I hung up in the middle of Lea explaining to me how much I owed (mates' rates) for the time they'd already spent on building the website.

I patted my father's dog's head.

I went up and remade my father's bed so I could sleep in it.

So what if they got into the studio?

En bee dee.

So what if Amelie played with the paints?

I'd want to, if I were her.

So what if something or someone happened to mess with or ruin a picture I'd been working on for over a year?

The poem wasn't going anywhere any time soon.

There'd always be more paint.

I could start again.

Imagine better.

Here was Martina Inglis in my head, old self and young self both at once spinning like a health and safety hazard on ice, dressed in white, blades for feet, little shavings of the ice flying away from them as she spins, arms high above her head like the neck of a swan. On either side of her, bookending her: Eden Pelf sitting on the cold surface and placing a tiny shard of ice that one of her mother's spins has flicked in her direction on her tongue, hesitantly, experimentally, see if she can taste it; Lea Pelf crosslegged and passionate, watching their mother spin but secretly altogether elsewhere, engrossed in the glare of the ice and in their own hand on that ice pressed hard against it as if to try, with determination, real resolve, how long they can bear to press themself up against a regulated coldness indifferent to warmth,

but what did I know?

I knew nothing really, about anything or anybody.

I was making it up as I went along, like we all are.

Alive v dead:

the next morning I called Martina Inglis's number.

Hi! she said. How lovely to hear from you. How're you? How's your dad sweet heart?

Could be worse. When is your family planning to leave my house? I said.

Could be worse here too, she said. We're staying as far away from Rory as we can, well, I am, but it's hard when there's only the one bathroom.

You could always all go home to your own lovely big houses, I said.

The last thing I want is covid all over my surfaces, she said.

You're a bunch of stupid self interested wankers, I said. That's my surfaces you're talking about.

Oh stop kicking off, Sand. You're safely elsewhere, she said.

I'm exceptionally lucky to have that luxury, I said.

Wish I was there, she said.

Thank God you're not. Where the bloody hell would I go then? I said.

Ha ha. Oh wait, she said. Eden wants a word.

Hi, it's Eden. Oh, he's okay. He says he feels worse than he's ever felt. But it's just jetlag.

I could hear a child coughing in the background.

Is that Amelie? I said.

Children don't get it, she said.

How are you? I said.

I've got a bit of a sore throat but apart from that I'm all right, she said.

How's Lea? I asked.

In your bed double-you eff aitch. That's working from home, remember, we've already done that one.

Double-you eff *em* aitch, I said.

What? Eden said.

Working from *my* home, I said. When are you leaving my house?

But her mother had taken the phone again and was speaking now.

By the way, Sand, I've been longing to tell you, I found the most beautiful thing that the Scottish poet Robert Burns wrote and it was about curlews.

I don't have it right here. But if I paraphrase a bit, he's writing a letter to charm this married woman, and he says something like whenever he hears a curlew on a summer morning it always reminds him he has a soul because his soul has lifted because he heard it, and then he says, what are we, are we machines so that whatever we hear is sort of meaningless? Or does hearing it and feeling something lift inside you mean, instead, that we're more than – and this is literally what he says – the *trodden clod*? Isn't that brilliant. What a life my old friend. We're so much more than the trodden clod, I'm telling you.

You're telling me, I said. Yes. That's a really beautiful thing you've found.

Next time I see you I'm going to find some suitable way to thank you. I'll take you to the museum and do a VIP tour, get them to show us the actual Boothby Lock. You'll see, it's like some iron version of King Midas just happened to touch a wall covered in ivy, then someone carved off and preserved a piece of its elegance for ever. And then, no getting out of it, Sand. I'm taking you skating.

Sure. We'll do those things. One day, I said. When you all leave my house. When this pandemic is over. Whichever of those takes longest.

Great, she said. I'm already looking forward.

Curfew

Hello hallo hullo.

It's comparatively quite a recent word. But like everything in language it has deep roots.

In all its forms, the dictionary says, it's a variant of a word from Middle French, hola, a combination of ho and la, making something like *hey there*. It might also connect to the old hunting cry, halloo! for when you sight what you're hunting and shout out with excitement as you start the chase. Or perhaps it might be closer to the sound of the word howl, like when Shakespeare uses it in Twelfth Night as one of the proofs of love when one character tells another that to prove this love she'd *halloo your name to the reverberate hills* till there's nothing else left in the air or the world but the name of the beloved.

Or maybe it comes from the Old English word

haelan, which is a very versatile verb that can mean to heal and to save and to greet all at once. Or from another Old English phrase altogether, one that means may you be hale, or may you be whole.

It's possibly also the Old High German word you'd've shouted if you were at the side of a river and needed to get a ferryman's attention. A form of it turns up in The Rime of the Ancient Mariner by Samuel Taylor Coleridge, a poem about the terrible act and ominous aftermath of the killing of a bird, the fate of the sailor who kills it and the deadly fate of his companions. First the bird comes playfully to their hollo! and brings good sailing weather. Then the mariner kills it. After that everything turns into deadly stasis in the poem. After it, shout hollo! all they like, no bird comes.

In any of its forms, hello can mean all these things. We say it to someone we've just met, it's a friendly and informal ritual gesture of greeting whether it's someone we know or someone we've never met before.

It can mean someone's surprised, or attracted, or caught off guard by something or someone, as in, hello, what's this? /who's this?

It can be a polite demand for attention; imagine you're standing in a shop and the person you want to serve you has gone through the back, say, so you shout it. It can also suggest there might be nobody there at all. For instance, you've fallen down a well and are stuck at the bottom of it looking helplessly up at the small circle of light that's the rest of the world and you're shouting it in the desperation and hope that somebody will hear.

Or you answer a phonecall and you say it and nobody answers or there's nobody there. So you say it again into the silence, more and more insistent each time,

hello?

hello?

Is anybody there?

Are you there and you can hear me but you're just not replying for some reason?

Can you help me?

Oh now *that* definitely caught my attention.

What's all this then?

What do you want?

Yes, I'm here.

Can you take me safely across in your boat?

Are we anywhere near land yet?

Please be well.

Please don't be broken.

Please get better, be safe.

I love you and I'm going to plaster the universe with your name and my love.

I'm on your trail and I'm coming after you.

Eh, hi.

Good to see you again.

Good to meet you.

Every hello, like every voice – in all the possible languages, and human voice is the least of it – holds its story ready, waiting.

That's pretty much all the story there is.

Round any telling of it, a deep green colour layered with grime and dust from all the seasons over a door in a wall, both the door and the wall invisible under the massive swath of ivy shifting its leaves in slight-breeze choreography, lit here and there by the brighter green of its newer leaves, the newest of these such small perfected leaf shapes already that it's both ordinary and mindblowing and then there are the little plant teeth like roots coming off the tendrils reaching for and holding to whatever surface they touch, dogged, firm, working to become more root than tendril, the whole thing fed by a taproot so deep and tough that, whoever or whatever tries to cut it back or dig it out, here it comes all over again one unfurled leaf at a time.

There were three at the door at curfew. They threw the door open. Wotcheer, one said. Get the legs, the other said. I'll do the dogs if there's trouble, the third said.

Then they did it.

If she wasn't good at her trade they wouldn't have. They did it to her because she knows a lot more than how to make a knife.

The girl is in the ditch where they dumped her. Now that it's morning she can see it's a ditch she's in.

Nails and then knives, they're the earliest easiest, how to sharp, how to blade. Nails are common-easy, never a waste of time to make them, always worth it, heat the rod, hammer the sides of the softened end while you turn it, keep the rhythm, down goes the end to a point. For the rich decorate the head of a nail like an acorn or spiral, sun, moon, shell, fruit. For everyone else a nail's a nail.

For a knife, if it's an all metal knife, take a forearm-length piece of layered steel and iron. Mark it at the centre. One half the blade, the other the handle. Start with the handle, heat the end, beat the sides, taper till it's as long as the beak of a long beaked bird, blunt its corners as you go so it won't hurt or annoy the hand that'll hold it. Draw it to a point. Hook the pointed end with soft hammer then round it into a closed loop, bend the whole handle into a soft V then gently into U. For the blade cut the metal away on the slant. Forge. Flatten and tease it. Forge. Back to the handle. Forge. Close it for comfort. Forge. Grind it. Work the blade till bright. Bury the knife in white heat for some hours, to harden. Oil it. Heat a stone to temper the spine. Grind clean and sharp.

Her head is full of nails and blades and the fire it takes to make them, bright red, the blood colour.

Orange flame for forging. White flame for the weld where a thing becomes one with another.

Worse things happen.

Worse things happen.

She let them in. They'd thumped her in the stomach, taken her hammer and held it above her head though they were decent in the end and hadn't hit her with it. Instead one held her down over the anvil, one had her, and the third watched, the witness.

They could all have had her there and then but they didn't. Because having her wasn't the point and they wanted her to know it.

She knows it.

She knows them all. Everybody knows them. Everybody will know what's happened.

Worse things happen.

They killed the dogs first because the dogs were growling. While they did it nails and knives were what were in her head. Knives take more thought so she thought knives keenly for most of the being had. When they were finished she played as dead as the dogs and they put her in a sack and dumped her, now she knows it was the moorfield they dumped her on, the sacking is her bedding in this ditch. God knows where the dogs got dumped.

She has five years apprenticed. Two more years to go. Those years can't happen now. It is law. Whether you chose to fuck or didn't makes no difference to law and that was the point of the being had. That's her brotherhood over.

Curfew. She was covering the fire, it's law to, when they came in.

She is thirteen years.

She is thinking to die.

Why not? This ditch is as good as a grave. Its sides are good and high. They go all the way up to what sky there is. It's a cold bed but it's soft enough. She could choose never to leave this ditch. She'll heap earth over herself as a coverlet.

The earth in your hair and your mouth is kinder, than.

She could lie here till she's what the weather will make of her one way or another one day soon enough whether she dies now or later. Weather will clean you well and creatures that are hungry will too and nothing wasted.

The sky and the earth and the rain and the teeth of creatures are kinder, than.

The filigree for the church door? never be finished now. Church doors need to be locked to keep the people both out and in, Ann Shaklock said. Churches like to flaunt their closedness. Even though the church didn't like Ann Shaklock it still gave the Shaklock forge the work. Then Ann Shaklock died, young to be dead people said, lung rot, the metal got into her, and a week is all it took till they wanted the forge and wanted her out of it, well, were they ever going to leave it to a girl? Even if every person in the whole place knows how good with horses. So much so that people came from places which have their own forges to Shaklock's instead to have Shaklock's apprentice do their horse's feet and health. And if a horse was particular and difficult they would still bring it miles.

Now that I'm down in this ditch am I still good with horses or not?

I'll lie in this ditch till I join Ann Shaklock.

I'll block my nose and mouth with moss and swallow moss till I stop breathing long enough to get me to her.

It's when she reaches a hand to the top of the ditch to see if there's mossy stuff on the surface that she senses the buzzard, the blink of cold through the weak warmth when it passes between her and the sun. She looks up, sees it hover then drop then come back up at an angle with something in its claws.

She heaves herself out of the ditch to look for moss.

She checks beneath her clothes.

She isn't bleeding now. She's sore though now. To move a limb, to breathe upright, hurts.

Then she forgets she's sore when she hears the call, something small somewhere over there in that longer grass.

In a hollowed bowl formed in it she finds a very young bird, duckling-like. But ungainly, pointy beak longer than duckling, falling over itself with its head too heavy for its body, and its feet, though they're big enough, not mastered yet.

She knows not to touch it.

She moves off and waits in the grass a far enough distance away.

But all morning there are no parent birds who come back to guard it.

We're the same, then, bird.

Bird pie for sale in the market square. That's your mother. Or foxes. Some foxcubs have eaten well. Did the hawk take your sister or brother? It took something. It's seen you too. It'll be back for you.

The bird is a little baby. It looks at her with a lit black eye, bright, a happy eye, eyes that have no fear in them at all. It is smiling though it doesn't know it is. Its head is a dark down cap and its downy body is so small that its feet are broader than its whole self.

It stops the chup-chupping noise when she settles next to it. It is so small she could cover it with just one hand, say a fox comes looking, or a kite, or that hawk comes back.

I can just as easily lie next to this hollow as I can lie in a ditch.

I don't have to join Ann Shaklock presently.

I can do this small guarding first.

She falls asleep in the sun.

When she opens her eyes the bird is deep in her armpit sleeping.

You're a rogue, bird, she tells the sleeping bird. Have you a trade? Have you any land that belongs to you? I'm richer than you now. Before, I had nothing. Now I have you.

She checks the nest for any eggs. There are no

more eggs. This kind of bird lays big eggs worth good money and if it *is* the kind of bird she thinks it is, a find of this bird, egg or hatched, can mean *very* good money. Its flesh, everyone knows, is pure and clean because this bird is known to eat nothing but air and is also known to be a bird that comes as a gift from God to befriend the pilgrims and it exists, the story goes, to weld the heaven to the earth. There are so many stories about this bird if it's what she thinks it is. The stories say it is a bird that likes books and even brings them in its beak to saints if the saints have dropped their holy books in water and they need retrieving or if the saints are short of something to say to people then this bird will be the messenger that brings them books full of things God would like them to say.

I could've turned over asleep, not known what I was doing and lain on it and crushed it.

Although she thought she already hurt all over this thought makes a different pain happen in her chest.

The bird wakes up.

It sits by her face with its beak wide.

Eats air is a lie. The bird wants fed and it wants more than air.

I'm not a bird, she tells it. I can't feed you.

What do they eat?

She stands up. The bird does too. It falls forward on to its chin over her feet.

She scrabbles about in the earth under the hedge. She unearths a red worm. She holds it out to the bird.

The bird waits. Then it takes it!

She goes back to look for another.

I'll need to eat too.

I could eat this bird. I could sell it for food.

She stands up again. The bird flurries about at her foot. She looks round the moorfield. She sees the smoke from the houses in the far distance. She turns to put that smoke behind her and she sets off walking.

But the bird she's left behind starts cheeping like a thief is stealing its purse. She hears herself laugh.

She comes back to the hollow, picks the bird up and puts it in the pocket of her apron.

Her hand coming out of her pocket again smells of metal.

That night she will creep back, climb the shade tree and go through the place in the roof that Ann Shaklock showed her that isn't known to anyone and is always easily opened. She'll tuck her own things into the apron pocket then put the baby bird back in, couched on top of them.

With her own tools she can journeyman if the places she goes or the people who might have food have any work that needs done.

*

The bird, she'll find out in the weeks to come, eats berries, all kinds. It eats soft things she can prise out of the shells stuck to the rocks at the shore. It eats all small life. It likes worms. It will eat grass if it has to, and grit and sand. It likes to eat a beetle and loves big-winged flies and little biting flies. Little fish, if she can catch them, it loves.

Soon it can catch all these creatures itself with its beak-tip, can break the living things out of their own shells, de-leg a crab and eat the legs last.

One day it brings her a very small fish and drops it by her foot.

The first time it meets with its own kind of bird she sees it disappear.

She thinks she'll never see it again.

But it comes back, runs back to her out of a group of its kind with its knees bent backward on its legs that look thin enough to be snapped by a wind with any force in it and its beak that looks like God kept going with the pen to see how long a beak He could get away with.

It learns from being with its own kind of bird how to swallow things, especially as the tip of its beak gets further away from the place in its head where its mouth is. It learns how to search and find things to eat not visible on the surfaces of the sand, grass, mud, water. It learns to speak bird words with its family and to fly by itself *and* with them.

She should chase it and be rough to it so it goes

and has the life it should be having. She should tell
it to be wild.

But it will hog her armpit till it gets too big for in
there and then hog her pocket till its beak is too
long and then, the size of a cat but thank God not
as heavy as a cat would be on a neck all the time,
it'll sit on her shoulder under her hair through
which, like through the gap in a rich house's
hanging silks, it will point its beak, its fishing rod,
its trident, tool of its trade, narrow as a finely
beaten curved and tapering line of iron and maybe
as strong.

But when she holds it in her arms she can feel its
bones so thin that the pain that's unlike any other
pain happens in her chest. This is the pain of the
thought of something painful happening to another
being. This is pain sensed or the thought of it
happening in another body by the body of the
person not feeling that same pain but feeling this
thing that's both pain and unlike pain instead.

The bird's feathers will now be beautiful. They'll
have the shape as if drawn on, on each of the
longer wing feathers, of the branches of a shrunken
pine tree or a set of arrow quills. On its head,
holding each eye, there's a slight mark, a > as if
inked then faded. It is very fetching.

The bird's family members will be wary of her.
They'll rush away from her.

But they'll learn she's not going to do them

harm, that she doesn't move much, that when she does move it's slowly and never a threat to them.

They'll grow to ignore her.

When they ignore her she is filled with pride because they are clever birds about what threatens them, like they're clever about the tides, they know when the water's coming in and going out and what good it'll do them either way. They know a richness in the muddy spaces.

But their trust has to be won by the hour. They're wise to people.

Like she is now too.

When they go wherever they're going in the sky together it's the shape of a V they make.

Her bird will watch them go, listening to them calling out their words.

The words that this kind of bird calls are said to be the calls of all the souls waiting in heaven to be born all shouting how keen they are to come to life. They sound like human words. What. What. What. Pearly. Pearly. Early. They don't mean those things. They aren't human words. So they can't un-mean either like human words can. The life in human words can be taken and beaten by careless working into badly made shapes averse to the life that's in them. Anything badly made or badly meant or badly given to another, she knows from her learning, will lead to common dishonour and deep shame.

In knowing this and in knowing the bird and its

ways, she's privy to an everyday other life, one she didn't have to die in a ditch to get to know. This other life is happening by itself alongside what people think life is. It has its own ways that like tendrils of an ivy form and thrive and layer and cloak themselves over themselves for safe keeping.

Privy to. Tendrils.

She writes these words in the sand now with a piece of stick because she can write her letters and do numbers as well as has learned the trade. All because of a flake of light. Ann Shaklock's husband Jack Shaklock had a boy working the forge with him when a spark from the forge flew out into the boy's eye and the boy missed the spike with the hammer, hit Jack Shaklock's right hand instead and crushed it past any healing.

Ann Shaklock took over the forge.

The local men were angry.

But Ann Shaklock knew it all already, she was good at it, her father'd been the smith, she'd been apprenticed to him, worked this place herself in the plague years when she couldn't be at school and then she'd married the smith Jack Shaklock on purpose to keep her father's forge.

One day the girl was standing in the street hoping for food but not out loud because if you ask for food and have no one to vouch for you it means jailed and branded and sent to sea to work tobacco.

A man saw her.

He asked her to hold his horse for him while Ann Shaklock shod it. He promised her a coin if she would.

This man was afraid of his own horse.

This was because the horse was trouble, everyone knew it. Everyone who had any money put a bet on that the horse would kick the little girl from the dead house to kingdom gone.

The girl, who was small, shorter than the length of the horse's legs, stood alongside the fine horse when the man took her to it and reached up and put her hands as high as they'd go. She touched where the horse's chest met its underneath.

The horse ignored her.

Then she stood alongside it up on the mounting block and reached to its shoulder. The horse turned its nose and nudged her head but gently and blew its grass breath into her hair, it was sweet, the breath, the mouth and nostrils soft.

She got down off the block and went towards its rear and the crowd in the marketplace shuffled away from the back legs when she went there because bucking and kicking were coming.

She stretched up and patted its flank.

The horse came all the way out to the smithy with her, following her like a lamb, Ann Shaklock shod it there without any trouble while the girl spoke to it and it listened with one ear cocked towards her.

The crowd, who'd followed at a distance, was full of people cheated. The ones who'd bet on the girl getting hurt wanted their money back. The ones who hadn't spent any money on anything also acted like they wanted money back.

Their noise didn't bother the horse.

Then the crowd went, the horse and his man were gone too, that horse bucking and kicking because he didn't like the man on his back. The girl hadn't been given a coin. The promise of a coin had been a lie. Then Ann Shaklock standing smoking her pipe at the door called the girl over and told her she had some work for her. The girl thought maybe Ann Shaklock would want her to look after the new baby. But the first thing Ann Shaklock did was take the girl to the heart of the forge, hand her the poker and pincers and stand her square on very close to the heat.

You know what clinker is? she said. No? It's the stuff in there that's lighter than coal and it sticks together under it and hinders the fire doing what you ask it to. A fire hates its clinker. Clinker hates its fire. Now. Here. See if you can find the hatred in there and hook it out for me so we can throw it away.

The girl poked the fire, looked deep into it, felt for the what might be clinker and fished the big and then the small bits of it out.

That's good, Ann Shaklock said. Those tools I gave you are yours now. They're your new hands.

Ann Shaklock was as strong as the tree next to the forge and sometimes even seemed as tall as it. She was beautiful with her hair roped at the back and hanging stuck to itself in clumps round her forehead at the front, all the skin hard and burned rough on her arms and hands and face.

She apprenticed the girl.

She went to see the overseer and signed the paper.

What happened to your father? she said. Your mother?

The girl told her how they were first sick then both dead in the bed together.

Were you sick too? Ann Shaklock said.

I sickened but am not dead, the girl said.

It's true, Ann Shaklock said. You're not!

Ann Shaklock gave her a pencil, a knife, and a thin piece of wood to start to learn on.

Letters and numbers come before the hammer or you'll ruin your hands and never be able to do them, she said.

Then she said, how do you know your numbers so well? You might be a scholar or musician already the way you know them. Who taught you them?

I don't know.

There was music in numbers, Ann Shaklock told her. You could unlock numbers and music was hidden in them like there was hammer music in where and how and when to hit a thing you're making and when to hit the anvil as you turn the thing. There were hammers and anvils deep in human ears, she said, because smithing is a kind of listening, and she told the girl about Pythagor who was the first to notice that a heavy hammer made one sound and a lighter a different sound and that all music might be to do with lightness and heaviness.

They keep us at our distance from their houses because of our music, Ann Shaklock said, and because we're a fearful people to them, dealing in fire as we do and in the changing of substances from one thing to another. They love us for our magic, and then when they forget their good sense they think we're doing black magic and they get scared and angry. But when my father played the anvil he was good enough to dance to. I don't have the gift like he did, but you I can hear it in. I'll train you like he trained me. The people might stop their complaining. They might welcome their houses shaking and their air full of the sound of us. But take care. They get angry at anything, everything. They think we have powers we don't. They need us so much for the making and the mending of things that them needing us makes them angry too. And be doubly careful, being what you are. They shout all the time it was a woman that made the nails for the crucifixion when her husband the smith refused to. As if a story's proof that we're fearful creations full of badness so they can burn us on our own forge if they choose. Take care what you make. Beauty can anger as well as please. Take care to keep things plain. Unless someone's paying you well to do different.

Every year Ann Shaklock remade her own clothes to fit the girl growing and there was an uncracked apron every season.

You have to be free in your movement or you'll hurt yourself. You have to be able to be quick. Leather makes you sweat. Linen is better for movement but it's costly.

She taught her how to read fire, how to deepen it, lessen it, make it right for what you're making, the fade and the growth of the glow, when to put what you're working back into the heat and when it's ready to take out, how to shift its temperature up or down with the bellows. How to work the bellows by foot on the pedal so that the baby in the basket hanging on the other side of the room from the heat and the smoke will be rocked to sleep by the ropes Ann Shaklock had tied across the roof like rigging, or be rocked into stopping crying anyway and either way work won't be interrupted.

Worse things happen at sea and in Virginia, Ann Shaklock told her when she burned herself. Say it after me, say it. Hold the burn in water, keep it there, lap water over it, that's even better, pour water on a bad burn, keep pouring it. Say it slowly as you pour it or lap it a hundred times, worse things happen, worse things happen, worse things happen at sea and in Virginia.

She taught the melting of the ore to get the sand out of the iron. The acrid smell was iron, the sweeter smell the steel. The best steel came from Flemland. Forest of Dean was iron. She taught her the persuading hit needed for decoratives and the hard hit for clean cutting. She taught her how to do the dawn fire and how to do the curfew.

One day a vagrant rogue was to be branded in the market. They came to Ann Shaklock to make the new brand. Ann Shaklock had the girl make it herself. She watched her fix the wooden handle well on the rod and showed her how to prepare and form the relief lettering and taught her how to make the sides of that lettering as clean as they could be made. That way less pain later, she said, and a cleaner heal for the poor person, and may the disgrace they've been made to suffer heal as cleanly.

As the girl made it Ann Shaklock told a story about how the letter they were making was born. It began as a bird. An Egyptian scriber drew a bird, its head, its wings, its body, its feet, like you look at a bird if it has its side turned towards you. Then that bird shape tempered, became a circle with a line straight down from it. Then it changed to a letter more like Y with a body below and arms held towards heaven. Then it purified itself down even further, it didn't need a body, just its arms supplicating.

That two divided things will come together and make just one thing.

That all closed things will open to the sky.

And that, Ann Shaklock said as she dipped the brand in the oil to finish it, is what the letter V means, and this brand, whomsoever it will burn, will mark as different from the others a wanderer, a vagabond, a person more free in this life than most of us can be and though they pay dear for their freedom God help them they walk free for all of us who can't.

Ann Shaklock knew the words from the other countries. Cur was short for cover, few was a word for fire. She knew because the nuns taught her, she'd been sent to them when she wasn't working the forge because her father had no son and thought her clever, and she was schooled by them till she was fourteen. Then she'd come back to work with him until he died, his arms and his face went blue black with the blood and bruises. He turned as black as iron in the forge, Ann Shaklock said. That was the plague tempering him.

Ann Shaklock smoked the pipe all day to keep the plague away.

*

She told the girl the stories about St Eloi and his cleverness with horses, his canniness at stretching his metals further than possible. That's how we eat, she said, and you're already good with both these things, horses and metals. What we do, she told the girl, is tend to the feet of horses and make coarse metal shine like precious metal. The foot of a horse is precious and the coarse can shine, d'you hear me? Anything unbending, send heat through it. The ungiving nature can be made to give. The fiercest earth, air, water, fire, all four, can be persuaded to work with us, like the horses do, if we're respectful of their powers and learn their languages.

When the girl was younger and settled in the dogs' bed with the dogs happed round her for sleep Ann Shaklock sat on the floor next to her and told tales of Vulcan, the god of all forges. She told her how he took earth and clay and heat and made a girl and how that girl went and opened the box that had all the world's evil in it and the evil flew out like hornets out of a smashed nest into the world and after she did this the box seemed empty but it wasn't because there was still the world's goodness in it down in the dregs of the badness.

There was not a good enough lock on that box, the girl said shaking her head.

Ann Shaklock laughed when she said this and so did Jack Shaklock who was across the house in the wall-bed, their laughing woke the baby, woke the dogs, one dog jumped in the air and another jumped out of the bed and stood bewildered in the middle of the room.

That was one story.

There was another about how Vulcan's mother was a goddess called June and though the month of June can be temperate the goddess really wasn't and she hated the baby Vulcan, she must've had her reasons to, I don't know what they were, but she did, so much so that she threw him off the top of her mountain. Her mountain was so high that the baby Vulcan fell down the side of it for three months, God knows how he didn't starve, he must've grabbed at herbs as he fell and when he finally hit the sea hot steam rose off it like hot metal in the cooling bucket. The fall into the sea had broken his leg when he hit it so hard but when he sank down to the bottom of the sea a broken leg wasn't such a hindrance and he rode a dolphin like a horse.

The girl liked this story.

There was the one about how that poor vagabond branded in the square here last year was on the beach next to the sea one day and he'd lit a fire and left it burning while he went to clean the meat to cook on it. That day Vulcan came up out of the sea to have a look around, he was pulled to the surface by a hundred horses of the sea which are much much smaller than our horses which is why he needed a hundred of them. They have white manes, you can see their manes in the waves. They don't need shoes, they use their tails for feet and you can't shoe a tail. Vulcan was on the shore limping along and he saw the fire. It was the first time he ever saw fire and he fell in love with the red in the embers.

So he found a big shell whose creature had moved on and he tucked a coal ember and a wood ember into the shell and took both back under the sea with him to a cave he knew where he could keep a fire going, I know it sounds unlikely but he did. And under the sea in his cave he learned how to read fire like you can, like I can, like Mr Shaklock can and like my father could.

First he made nails and spikes and knives. Then he made a sword. Then he made a plough and furrowed the sand on the seabed and grew sea corn and sea oats. He made a pony-trap out of gold and he collected his hundred horses round it and they pulled him up and down the long road at the bottom of the sea. Then he made necklaces and rings and bracelets and head-dresses and little charms on dainty chains, and he gave them to the mermaids who were very delighted with them.

Ann Shaklock told how Vulcan is to blame for all the vanity in mermaids and how one of the vain mermaids, who'd fallen for a man she'd met on the shore and left the sea behind for him, met June the mother of Vulcan in the upper world of gods and people and when June saw what beautiful frippery the mermaid was wearing she wanted some the same. So she sent an ambassador under the sea to find this master metalworker.

Vulcan laughed when he heard who it was who wanted his decoratives. He set to work making a throne out of the world's most precious metals and he presented this beauty of a throne to the lord ambassador and the ambassador had it heaved up out of the sea on to the land then made five hundred duty boys and duty girls carry it to the top of the mountain. That goddess thought it was the finest furniture she'd ever seen. She ran across the room to sit in it – and when she did that the throne's arms came alive, its legs came alive and the arms pinned her in it so she couldn't move and the legs did a dance with her in the throne, tossing her about in the palace for days like she was tied to a horse gone mad.

June's husband, the overseer of the gods, was so angry that he dashed all the duty boys and girls who'd brought it back down the mountain and right down into the sea where they would've drowned if they hadn't been picked up by our own overseer and put on the boat to the Americas to be set to work in the tobacco fields and to be honest, girl, drowning might've been better luck. Then he sent a message down to Vulcan under the sea.

195

If Vulcan would free June from the throne, he'd give Vulcan another goddess, the goddess of love, to be his wife. And in an instant he –

Jack Shaklock called from the wall-bed.

Ann. For Jesus sake. It's well past curfew. Let the girl sleep. Let the dogs sleep. Let Vulcan sleep. *I* need to sleep. Come to bed now.

The girl lay in the dark and thanked St Eloi and Vulcan and the church-God and all the gods and stars.

She had had no family and no home. But now she had this new-beaten likeness of both.

When you hammer a lit place on metal it's light itself that comes off it in flakes. Each flake as it moves is time moving on the power of its own waning.

That's what I want, the girl thought. Time taking the shape of air, only alive till it's gone. Like when a star travels like an arrow across a sky in summer.

Precious stone is mud, compared.

A star can be an arrow.

One thing can become another.

They say a soul is a fixed thing and can't be changed.

But all things *can* change or *be* changed, by hands and elements. Old horseshoes will be melted to make new horseshoes. Weapons into tools for the fields instead. Tools for the field into weapons again.

It was the difference between the ore and the

iron, the old life and the new life, pig iron and wrought. She was not a duty girl like the poor orphaned jailed girls swapped for money or tobacco then sent off in the ships into the endless.

She had a bed that was warm even in winter and dogs to warm her in it. She had food, a roof, a trade.

She had a friend who smiled at her in church, Christine Gross from the farm, they went walking one Sunday, Christine Gross was older, very pretty, had a way of slipping an arm through the girl's arm as they were walking through the empty marketplace so that the girl felt known, more, she felt seen, and liked.

She had a mistress-master.

She was good not just with horses.

When Ann Shaklock first saw what she could do with filigree she ran across the yard and woke Jack Shaklock from his midday sleep to come out to the forge and see it too.

After that she set her to do all the decoratives, the high orders, rich hinges, rich nails, church doors.

Then the baby died of coughing.

Then Jack Shaklock died.

Then Ann Shaklock died.

Then there was a week in which the men who wanted the forge for themselves were biding their time before they came to take it.

Then it was curfew.

When the girl knocks on a door now and the door opens people see a vagabond and a thief. As soon as they see her they know they don't know her.

There's a lot of being looked at like she's a liar and Egyptian, the occasional milk or porridge or egg given at the door, mostly out of fear. There's a lot of closing doors, a lot of people trying to steal her tools from her, but only one time when a man tries to steal the bird and it only takes that chase and escape for the bird not to sit on her shoulder any more when she's anywhere near the world of people and to start travelling separate instead, alongside her, at a distance, catching her up when she settles in whichever hedge or hole in the ground they'll sleep in that night.

If anyone approaches them when they do find

somewhere they can get some rest, the bird wakes her to warn her with its *what what what* coming through its chest and into hers.

But the world with people in it is a kind of filth compared to this afterlife she did not actually need to die to find.

So as long as there's something to eat and it's not yet autumn, or cold, she's not yet a person in need of a welcome near or from people.

*

One day there's a fair happening in the town the girl is passing. There will be a lot of food around on the ground. Drunk people have no idea what they're eating or not eating.

People have gathered round a platform to watch the juggler. The juggler is a woman dressed like a sailor and she is throwing knives in the air and then catching them and throwing them again, all without cutting herself. Eight knives. As she catches the eighth, takes a bow and rises from it with the eight blades fanned in her hand, the juggler-sailor, who must have seen her approaching over the field and seen the bird fly off her and away, points at the girl and says,

now this fine bird-girl will sing her song. Won't you my darling?

I do know a song, the girl says.

She gets up on the platform.

She sings what Jack Shaklock taught her about the blacksmith and men's deceit. When she's sung its last line about living for ever the people round the platform roar. They start throwing coins. She picks one up off the planks and looks at it. She'd forgotten about coins. She hasn't seen or held a coin since they dumped her in the ditch.

Sing it again! the people are shouting.

The juggler gets back on the platform and stands beside her, takes her hand, makes her bow like they're working together. Then the juggler tells the people watching to *bring this juggler anything they choose, anything at all*, and after the bird-girl sings to them one more time, whatever it is they've brought her she'll juggle with it.

A woman holds out her baby. Juggle with this!

In twenty years' time I will, the juggler calls back.

When the laughter dies down the girl sings the song again. Even more people come. They sing the parts they know. At the end they throw more money at her.

Sing another!

I don't know another.

At the front of the platform there's the pile of things the people have brought for the juggler to juggle: a broken pot, a spoon, a broken piece of scythe. A ball made of rags, a rusted key, the handle from a churn, a wheel, a bucket. As she gets down after her song the girl takes the broken scythe piece and weighs it in her hands.

I want this, she says to the juggler. If no one else wants it or its owner doesn't want it back.

It'd take skill to keep just four of those things, never mind all of them, all their different shapes and weights completely new to her hands in the air like that and in a rhythm that stays steady against the oddness of the pieces. Never mind the dipping down to pick up and toss a new piece in the air with all the other pieces still above her in their rising falling arc.

This juggler would keep a good forge, the girl thinks.

I kept you your blade, the juggler says with her arm round the girl's shoulder after the juggling. We'll go and eat some of our money, come on, Strange News, I'll carry you.

It's because of the words in the song she sang. Strange news is come to town. Strange news is carried. Strange news flies up and down. The girl doesn't sleep with the bird that night. She sleeps in a pub leaning on the juggler whose arms and wrists and hands, she sees, are all scars and weals from the sharpness of the throwing-knives, and with others leaning on her.

It is like when the bird is with its own kind.

The next morning the traveller players wake early

and are on the road early because there'll be trouble otherwise.

The juggler says,

come and do the fairs with us for the rest of the summer. You'll win them every time, singing like that. I know songs. I can tell you the words for them. You could make enough to pay through winter.

It's far from winter right now. The girl knows this'll pass as fast as the sparks off metal do. But when she comes out of the pub door into the light with the others she sees something moving in the high teasel across the road and it's the bird.

We have a new story to play to people, the juggler says. Come and be a boy player. You could play a girl who goes mad at her father's murder and gives people different herbs and tells them what they mean.

Then what happens? the girl says.

Then she drowns herself, the juggler says.

The girl laughs.

I'm not that, she says.

You can be it and still be you, the juggler says. We'll teach you.

The girl promises to meet them further up the road. She waves her hand when they reach the bend in the path. But as soon as she turns away she's on her own path.

She's going to mend this scythe. Then it will be worth a lot more and she'll sell it.

Then she'll find the bird, hide the coins she'll make today with the ones from yesterday somewhere for the winter. Then it's back to the moors where the bird needs to be.

She asks a woman slapping washing against a stone which direction to take for the smithy.

She walks to the edge of the town though there's no smoke visible.

The forge isn't even lit.

It's well past six!

So she crawls through a window at the back of the place, a small window but she's thinner than it, and lights it with moss and sticks and her firestones. She looks for the place this smith keeps the offcuts. She sorts through the pieces. Her hands are happy to be back in the heat and they do the work without her even having to ask them.

Furious! He comes running at noon, she can hear him coming through her own hammer music. He crashes through the doors with his hand raised and a piece of iron in it to hit a thief and usurper with.

Then he sees her.

Small girl.

He stops.

He takes the piece she's working from her. He examines the place where the old blade meets the new-made blade. Then he looks at her again.

Are you the horse-healer? he says. From Shaklocks?

What if I am? she says.

They said you were dead, he says.

I'm not that, she says. I'm living in happy vagabundance, though occasionally hungry and cold.

She can see from his face he is not a man who likes these words. Not every smith is a Shaklock.

Perhaps he lost horses to Shaklocks because of her.

Too known is much worse in some places than not known. Now they'll learn in her town that she's still alive and those men who thought they'd killed her will come to try to do it again.

The smith makes her take off his apron. He takes her by the shoulders to a door in a tall house in the heart of the town. They wait while the locks get unlocked one after the other all the way from the top of the door to the foot.

You're with the travelling players, the overseer says. You sang the strange news.

He looks haggard, like he's drunk and was a moment ago still asleep.

Then she recognizes him from the fair.

He's the man who gave her a small coin and expected her to fornicate.

She'd looked at the coin in her hand then held out her other hand as if to take his. He'd put his hand out and she'd taken the hand, turned its palm upward, opened it and put the coin he'd handed her back into it. She'd closed his fingers round it and told him she wasn't for sale.

Fuck you to hell then, the man (she now knows is the overseer) had said. Rather fuck anyone or anything in hell than you, she'd said and the juggler and her travelling friends had closed a circle round the girl and laughed him off.

It turns out, the overseer says to the smith now over the girl's head, that the travellers this girl is with are wanted for several kinds of sedition.

It turns out they've been inciting trouble and violence telling people about the poor law being a law to keep people poor. There was nearly a riot in the market square of the workers from the farms grumbling about what they're paid, or at least the ones who didn't get drunk enough or fucked enough were grumbling, no one fucked enough or drunk enough cared so much.

Fucked enough.

The girl knows she's in trouble.

She's one of their tribe, the overseer says.

No, she's no itinerant, the smith says. She's trained as a brother. She knows the skills.

I'm not from a tribe, she says. I met them yesterday, and by chance, and they were kind to me. And I can tell you both myself what the tale-teller said last night verbatim.

Verbatim's not a word they expect from her. They both stare at her like she's shocking.

And how well and persuasive, she says, and how angry any people will be about it here today whose power has been questioned by what truths he spoke.

The man she is calling eloquent, the juggler's friend, the tale-teller of the players, had been dressed in the women's clothes still, in which he'd been playing the story to the crowds at the fair about the woman who travels across a river to try to wake the spirit of a dead child she's heard is buried there.

In this story a woman is looking for her own dead child. She is so desperate to find him that she crosses the country from side to side raising the spirits of all the dead and gone children to see if any of them is her boy. She's not yet found him. She's near mad with the looking and not finding. But the children's spirits when she raises them have soared into the sky crying their thank-yous down to her like birds.

The man on the platform became a woman beating a stick on flat beaten bronze. The spirit of the child will rise to the sound of the beating. The woman crosses a river on a boat with a ferryman and a holy man, both of whom fear this woman is mad, to a place where a child is under the ground. This time it is her child.

It nearly kills her to see him rise up dead out of the ground.

But the child doesn't stop rising, he rises and rises into the air and floats there like a sun above everything.

The people at the fair had gone wild for this story. They'd lost a lot in the plague year. They cried at the end and stamped their feet. They followed the travellers to the pub afterwards, caught up in the story like something had melted all their bodies into one body.

At the pub the tale-teller stood on a table still in the woman's clothes and he spoke to the people there with words coming through him as naturally as water from a source. Your wages are low on purpose so that you can't prosper from working. It's prosperous for some people to keep other people starving. You make them rich by it. But what if you withheld your work so that the people you work for could learn the work's worth? And why is it a crime for you or me to want to move from one place to another place? And why is it a crime to have nothing? These aren't crimes, he said, and this isn't a story in which we can live freely.

Now, next day in the overseer's hall, the smith is looking at his feet and the overseer is looking at the girl and listing the letters over her head with which she can be burned.

For sedition. Roguery. Vagrancy. Affray.

But look, the smith says.

He goes over to the table where the overseer's servant has placed everything belonging to the girl, her tools, her money. He picks up the scythe blade and presents it to the overseer, points to the mended places on it. The overseer comes to the table and flicks his hands around the girl's things. He picks up the hammer and weighs it. He takes it, the pincers and the firestones and holds them out to the smith like he wants the smith to take them in his hands, which the smith does. The smith holds the girl's things, looks at them like he doesn't know what to do with them.

The overseer picks up the mended scythe, puts it down behind the woodpile next to the fire. He's keeping it.

The girl can see now that her money's also gone from the table.

She doesn't care. She knows other worlds.

The tools were stolen from you, the overseer says. She's a thief too.

No, the smith says. They're her tools. They belong to her.

They're yours now, the overseer tells him.

The smith puts the things in his hands down on the floor. He steps back from them.

Take them, the overseer says.

You should, the girl says to the smith. Someone should get the use of them.

The smith shoots the girl a shamed look. She gives a slight shake of her head.

Worse things happen.

*

The overseer keeps her in a cellar for three days. But he doesn't dare touch her.

Good.

After three days in the dark he has her thrown by his manservant into the back of an open cart and delivered all the miles back to her old place to be dealt with. It's the law. Many of the people here look amazed she's still alive when they see her driven through the place sitting up rope-tied in the back of the cart. She's meant to be dead.

Word goes round that she's a kind of risen avenging saint-child.

Something like that can go either way for her.

Also, she speaks too much for a woman. She's been trained in the ways of men, which is a ruination. She's a discord bringer. Rumour says she walks about in the world with a bird on her shoulder, which gives rise to a lot of devilry rubbish.

But while she's locked in the back room of the bakery, which is where they hold the people waiting for judgement to be passed and announced, the baker's daughter brings her plenty of things to eat.

Other people bring gifts for her and pass them anonymously under the gap at the bottom of the locked back door. The lock would be piss-easy to pick. But what'd be the point? Flowers, one at a time, come under the door through the gap. Wool clothing and blanketing, flattened and persuaded through.

Blinded is another thing she can be, if they want, by them holding a hot brand near her eyes.

That woman there, she thinks as she's led through the crowd to the judgement, I hammered out her man's pain in his back with my hands when she brought him to the forge. I helped them over there too with the child who had the sick legs, I was bringing him the cooling water for half a year and look, he's nearly as grown as me now and looking pretty strong.

She knows the hoof of every horse, knows the horses by sight, still, and maybe the men at the Shaklock smithy now are less good with these people's horses' feet.

She is this town's good worth, lost.

That can go either way for her too.

Then they read the judgement:

and she isn't to be sent for witch trial thank God. So she won't be hanged or tied to a stake and set fire to.

She isn't to be sent to the tobacco fields. Thank St Eloi.

All that happens is she's locked in the stocks for one day and night.

In the stocks she's abused by no one, not even the drunks, because people don't want to anger a risen avenging saint-child.

Then she's pulled to her feet and taken, before noon next day, which is market day, and bound at the wrists in front of the crowd with thin iron bands made by Ann Shaklock and burned at the collarbone by the overseer's son with the V of a brand she knows as soon as she sees it is the one she made herself.

The overseer's son looks grim as he does it.

A lot of women in the crowd turn to look away when he does, which is a sign of public disagreement.

There's no general cheering and laughing, which there usually is at such entertainments.

This visible dissent means she knows now to get herself out of here as fast as she can or she'll be bound to get the blame for something she isn't to blame for, so they can do this all again with proper enjoyment as a taking of revenge on not being able to enjoy it enough the first time or having been made to feel bad about it happening at all.

When they free her hands she takes her burn straight to the well. But it hurts too much to reach over to pull up the water.

Three girls push through the crowd to help her.

She lies down flat on her back on the ground and tells them what to do.

One pulls the bucket up and pours the water into the pots. While the others pour the water on the burn the first pulls more water up to fill the emptied pots again.

One of the girls is Christine Gross.

This is my cousin, Christine Gross says pointing to the girl hanging much of herself over the side of the well to drop the bucket. And this is my sister.

Christine Gross and her sister sit with her on the wet ground in the spilled and spilling water and pour water on the burn until after the people go home and the overseer's men come to move them on. They go to the Gross farm. But Christine Gross's father says she's a witch and she can't come into the house.

Christine Gross takes her to the stable instead where the horses know her, they nod to her, they should, she's helped shoe them seasonally every year of near half her life. Christine Gross slices the onions and places the pieces on the burnt place. She and her sister and cousin sit with the girl under the legs of the grey horse Thunderclap and teach her, until they're forced to go back into the house, the words of the song about the burning of that town to ash back in history nearly twenty years ago long before any of them was alive.

She leaves as soon as the light's up. She finds a

cloth with two pies and seven apples tied inside it waiting for her at the farm gate.

As soon as she gets far enough off the road the bird appears, wings wide, silent, coming towards her under the sky and over the top of the harvest.

The wolf's at the door, though. Autumn's coming now and that's winter already in its arms.

One evening she waits in the dusk for the new smith at Shaklocks to do curfew and cross the yard to that old house where Ann Shaklock told her the stories of St Eloi and Vulcan, and Jack Shaklock taught her the song.

When the new smith sees her there in the shadows his face drains of colour and he bolts like a rabbit, runs all the way down the street.

Good.

The next day she walks to the town where she'd sung the song at the fair. The smithy is one of the first buildings she gets to. She waits off the road for this smith's curfew.

When he comes out of the smithy and sees her waiting he makes a sign to her that he's seen her.

He turns and unlocks the smithy door again, goes in and shuts it behind him. When he comes back out he's carrying things in his arms.

He crosses the road to her. He gives her back her hammer, her pincers and her firestones.

Do you want a job? he says.

I don't, she says. Thank you.

I'll take you on, he says.

It's kind, she says. No thank you.

Come and work here whenever you need to, he says. While I'm here you're welcome.

I won't, she says. Thank you.

She steps back off the road into the trees.

She's as free as the bird now.

She can go anywhere so long as she can also survive it.

She has a new song too, to sing, about the town in flames. It's just a song but it's about what fire can do and what's worth what when fire takes something and burns it to nothing but ashes and she can sing it like that's what she herself is, fire, she can send heat through it blazing bright then dark.

What happens next?

Does she go and find the players?

Does she follow the route to where the local fairs are still left in the year to find them playing their story in the market squares or the fairfields to people in exchange for money, food, a sleep in the warm?

Do they give her a part in that story they told her about?

The poor mad girl who's ruined by revenge and loss.

The young man on fire with what he can't change and with whether to live or to die.

When she fights the villains with the sword on the platform does that crowd at the fair go crazy with delight at what a good swordsman she is?

Probably, since she's always handled her tools of the trade like extra hands added on to her already skilled hands and now she knows the uses and skills of a long very strong beak to a thin-boned bird.

Does the bird still follow her at the safe distance through the summer months when she's in the more peopled world? or does it happily slip away at last into the world of other birds?

Does she leave the peopled world in the colder months to go and stand on a strand where the birds like her bird are congregated, to see if there's one that'll lift its head, turn its head, step out of the company and come towards her, fearless?

I'm not going to tell you what happened in the end to the girl, except that she went the way of all girls.

Same with the bird, other than that in the end it went the way of all birds.

If any of this ever happened, if either of them ever existed.

One way or another, here they both are.

Back in the 1930s in Ireland for this brief spark of a moment now:

the child who'll be my mother has arrived at the doctor's house at last. She knocks at the huge closed door.

Someone opens door after door on the other side of the closed door then opens the outer door.

It's a housekeeper.

She looks down from the top step at my mother rocking from foot to foot.

What do you want?

We're needing the doctor for my sister please.

Have you money?

I've no money.

The housekeeper tells her the doctor is eating his dinner and can't be disturbed. She says she'll pass the message on to the doctor.

By the time my mother gets home her sister is dead.

That doctor comes the next day in the late afternoon. He tells my mother's mother and father that if they tell anyone he didn't come out immediately to attend to their girl he'll report them as rebels to the authorities.

Two days later the bill for this doctor's visit arrives at their house.

It's my father who tells me that last piece of story.

I didn't know it before now.

He tells me it haltingly, in pieces, and like he's been waiting to.

I'm on my phone, holding it up, visiting him in hospital virtually from his own kitchen. A doctor in a mask and a face-shield speaks to me first. She says he's not out of the woods yet but that things look much brighter. I thank her. Then Viola in her mask and face-shield props the hospital iPad up in front of him. I thank her. I thank them for everything because any of this and all of this is miraculous.

Now he's speaking to the iPad, to me, through a mask, about a history this close to me that I didn't even know I had.

But *were* they rebels, then? I ask him after he tells me.

Were –? he says.

He closes his eyes, screws them up. He's not good yet with questions.

I flinch at my own stupidity. I take my phone and show him the dog in her basket again instead.

Desperate for a walk, I say. I'll take her as soon as I can.

Still at mine, then, he says. Good. Make yourself home.

This is how we started our conversation some minutes ago, me showing him the dog in her bed, the dog hearing him, rousing herself then looking blank at the phone, him saying, you're still at mine, that's nice, me telling him about the unexpected visitors I have at my own house and him saying,

hospital me. Hospitable you. Stay at mine. Make yourself home. Tins in the garage. Tuna, beans, corn. Help yourself. Bacon. Soup and mince. The freezer. Do the dishes. Do them properly. Check they're clean. Wipe down. Sideboard. Do it as you go.

I promised him I would wipe all the surfaces clean and told him I'd be in to see him as soon as I was sure I was negative, and he said,

negative. Isolated. Yes. My fault. I'm to blame. Not your mother. I was the wrong man. The wrong time. Hopeless. My fault.

Don't talk rubbish, I said.

We'd no choice, he said. Your mother especially. She'd no choice.

That's when he told me in bits of broken sentence the story of my mother and the doctor.

Now he squints at where he can see me on the screen, which means he's looking down and off to the side of me rather than at me, and he shakes his head and says,

away with the fairies.

You're back now, I say.

Dreamed you were here, he says. You told me words.

That was real. I did. That wasn't a dream, I say.

Then I was on a bird, he says. Or was it a word. Hung on it for dear life. Holding its neck. Dear life! High above trees we went. Oh, marvellous. I could see the roofs of, of. You know. Houses I'd made. Saw them from above.

Viola appears on the screen of my phone too.

Two more minutes, Mr Gray, she says. Two more minutes, Sand.

Tell me, my father says.

What would you like me to tell you? I say.

His eyes look bewildered again. My chest hurts to see it. So I tell him about the good weather and how everybody is acting like lockdown never existed, and that when I was driving around on one of the sunniest days yet I drove past the park and it was as full of people as it would be if no virus had ever happened, and that as I'd passed the Co-op I'd seen on the pavement a young woman come shooting out of the doors of the shop running so fast and in such a flimsy skimpy top that one of her breasts broke loose from her clothes and bounced up and down as she ran, she was running like an Amazon maiden, she was full of glee, she had a bottle of wine in each hand and behind her, too far behind her to catch her, a security man and he was running like crazy too.

My father barks so big and sudden a laugh that Viola comes running over to check he's okay.

I'll come and see you as soon as I know I'm clear to, I tell him.

He nods in his mask then Viola waves. The screen freezes on her waving hand and his eyes next to it looking down, as if not at me at all, though to him what he's doing is looking as at me as he can.

The story goes:
at exactly 8.35 every morning since we came to my
father's house my father's dog has gone to sit at the
front door where she whines with one paw up on
the old scratched place and scratches more of the
varnish off on to the mat.

This morning when she goes to sit there I fetch
the lead and open the door.

She bounds out and waits for me at the garden
gate. Then she bounds to my car in the loading bay,
she knows which car it is. She sits waiting next to it
on the pavement.

Whenever I take a corner the wrong way, go left
when she wants me to go right or right when she
wants me to go left, she barks until I turn the car
around and go the way she wants. I start to judge
which way to turn by watching the turn of her head

and the angle of her ear. When we get to the street by the river she snorts and stands up in the passenger seat wagging her tail and I know it's time to stop.

I put the lead on and let her out.

She pulls me towards the common.

She walks the edge of the cattle grid at the gate between the street and the park with a dainty placing of her paws so no paw falls through the grid. Then she sits down on the path and looks at me and I understand I'm to let her off the lead.

Joyful dog running across grass.

I walk the path myself under the trees with all their leaves open. The colour of things hits me like something I've lacked. The river, clay-colour close up, sky-colour far off, widens and curves, like assurance, like something going its own road, an open road lit by the light it catches and sends back out from itself.

How have I lived here all these decades and never been here and seen this place before? I know, because of a temp job a couple of years ago when I filled in for someone on leave at the council and saw the number of applications from companies who wanted to cover the common in houses and flats in just the fortnight I worked there, that this common is the town's plague pit, where they mass-buried their dead seven hundred, six hundred, five hundred years ago.

Here we are today on the surface of things.

A church bell tolls the distance.

I stop to read the Combined Sewage Overflow warning notice.

Swans, so many everywhere; two pass on the water shepherding six small cygnets. Further down the river a couple of swans are sitting in the river both holding, what *is* that, dark against the white tailfeathers? is it a foot? they're each holding one foot up and out of the water, are they warming their feet in the sun? A man wearing a broad brimmed hat is sitting on a bench playing chords on a guitar. A swan is standing on the other side of the path. It's watching and listening to the man play.

Woodsmoke rises from the chimney of a riverboat. The pleasure the scent of it gives me takes me by surprise. Further along the bank in a gap between the boats a man is fishing. Slightly further along from him a grey heron, as if with the man but keeping politely out of his way, is standing watching the place where the man's fishing line meets the surface of the water. There are magpies shouting. There are crows, moorhens, seagulls shouting. There are people walking dogs, people taking the tarmac path or following their noses along grass paths. There's a rope swing hanging off a tree and a barer patch that curves round the tree made by all the people who've swung on it. There are cows grazing across the common. They're all facing the same way. Animal magnetism. They wander across the tarmac in front of people on bikes, in front of the joggers; their eyes are big, gentle, ready to be mistrustful, their spirit is something between bullish and mischievous and their heft, up close, is magnificent.

My father's dog is barking across the grass, jumping at somebody on a bike and now running back towards me still barking the almost cheeky-sounding high yelpy string of barks, and the person on the bike is coming towards me too, cycling alongside.

She's young, and bright, the person my father says hello to on his dogwalks.

She stops at the right distance. She doesn't get off her bike. She stays on the seat, puts one foot on the grass to balance herself.

Are you walking Shep? she says.

I am, I say.

Where's Shep's owner, I mean his usual walker? she says. Is he okay?

He's my father, I say. He's in hospital. Not the virus.

Thank God, she says. But oh no. Is he, is he, okay?

Not out of the woods yet, I say. Under observation.

Then I add,

heart stuff. But he's much much better than he was.

I've been worried, she says. I've been watching for Shep most days, Shep always chases my bike when I go past, for fun I mean, we always have a laugh, I love it when a dog laughs, and I was worried not to see him or your father and that's weeks now, because I always see them, even on the days when the weather's really bad, we always shout a hello to each other.

Yes, I say.

Will you pass on my best wishes to him? she says.

Course I will, I say. Thank you.

She turns her wheel, points the bike towards the path away from town. She calls over her shoulder as she goes.

Tell him hello from me.

I'll tell him, I say.

She heads off swift as a swift.

But then she brakes, stops, balances on one foot again on the path and turns her head to call something else to me over the heads of other people walking the common this morning.

And to you too, she says. Good to meet you. Hello.

I call it back.

Hello.

Acknowledgements and thanks

Biggest thank you goes to the NHS and
to everyone who works in it.
We're lucky to have them, and we all know it now,
and anyone who beleaguers or messes with them
does us all an immense damage.

A number of textual and online resources
helped in the writing of this book,
especially texts by David L MacDougall
and Marcia Evans.

Thank you, Simon.
Thank you, Anna.
Thank you, Lesley B.
Thank you, Lesley L, Sarah C, Ellie,
Hannah and Hermione
and everyone at Hamish Hamilton and Penguin.

Thank you, Andrew,
and thank you, Tracy,
and everyone at Wylie's.

Thank you, Xandra, ever just the best.
Thank you, Mary.

Thank you, Sarah.